"I'm the best man," he said, slowly. "And you're the maid of honor..."

"Of course." She tried to laugh it off, but it came out stilted as she tried to control the heat bubbling within her. "I'd hate to keep you from your date, though."

"I didn't bring one."

"She couldn't make it?" Penny fished just a little, knowing that if there was a *she*, Penny needed to shut down this attraction. She didn't mess with taken men.

"There isn't one." He looked over her shoulder briefly before returning his gaze to her eyes. "What about your date? Won't it make him jealous that I'll have you in my arms most of the night?"

"If he existed, it probably would." The men she hooked up with were always free agents and never more than that. "I guess that means I'm yours tonight."

Dear Reader,

In *Father by Choice,* Penny Montgomery was introduced as Maggie's best friend. I always knew there was a history with her and the youngest brother, Luke Ward. There were also unresolved issues between Luke and Sam, the oldest brother. It wasn't until I was curious about the surname Montgomery that I discovered that I'd stumbled upon a combination of last names that was really familiar. By then the first book had already been published, so I was stuck with Penny Montgomery and Luke Ward. I consider it a happy accident. It certainly made me laugh. I hope you enjoy Luke's book, and I look forward to getting Sam's book out there for you, too.

It's not easy to write a book, and it takes a family to make it happen. My editors, agent and all the brilliant people at Harlequin make the final product the best it can be. My critique partners, both old and new, help me brainstorm to take a vague idea and form a story worth telling. The organizations I've joined help me find other writers who encourage me to fill the well when I feel drained. The readers— without you I wouldn't worry over every word, every sentence, every chapter. I want you to have the experiences I have when I read a good book. Thank you for making my dream come true.

Best wishes and happy reading,

Amanda Berry

One Night with the Best Man

—

Amanda Berry

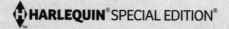
HARLEQUIN® SPECIAL EDITION®

Recycling programs
for this product may
not exist in your area.

ISBN-13: 978-0-373-65846-6

ONE NIGHT WITH THE BEST MAN

Copyright © 2014 by Amanda Berry

This edition published by arrangement with Harlequin Books S.A.

For questions and comments about the quality of this book, please contact us at CustomerService@Harlequin.com.

® and TM are trademarks of Harlequin Enterprises Limited or its corporate affiliates. Trademarks indicated with ® are registered in the United States Patent and Trademark Office, the Canadian Intellectual Property Office and in other countries.

Printed in U.S.A.

Books by Amanda Berry

Harlequin Special Edition

Father by Choice #2262
One Night with the Best Man #2364

Silhouette Special Edition

L.A. Cinderella #2052

Other titles by this author available in ebook format.

AMANDA BERRY

After an exciting life as a CPA, Amanda Berry returned to writing when her husband swept the family off to England to live for a year. Now she's hooked, and since returning to the States she spends her days concocting spicy contemporary romances while her cats try in vain to pry her hands off the keyboard. Amanda moved from the Midwest to the southeast coast with her husband, two children, two cats and a beagle–Jack Russell mix. For more about Amanda and her books, please visit www.amanda-berry.com.

To my husband and children,
thank you for helping me follow my dream.

Chapter One

"How's the bride?" Penny Montgomery stepped into the church dressing room, where her best friend since childhood, Maggie Brown, was getting ready to walk down the aisle. This church, one of five in the small town of Tawnee Valley, was the one Maggie's mother had dragged Maggie and Penny to when they were growing up.

"Nervous. Excited. Trying to remember to breathe." Maggie hadn't stopped smiling. Her gown was lovely and simple. Classically A-lined styled with no train. Her light hair was pulled up in a loose knot with tendrils left to play around her neck. She looked stunning and had the truest heart of anyone Penny had ever known.

"You look beautiful," Penny said. "Your mother would have loved to see you like this."

Maggie nodded. Tears sparkled in her eyes but they didn't fall. For years, Penny and Maggie had been each other's rock. Now Maggie had found her dream man and was forming a family. Penny had Maggie and that was enough family for her.

"Mom would be happy."

A lump formed in Penny's throat and she coughed to clear it. "Brady wanted me to give you this."

She held out the little gift-wrapped box.

"Thank you, Penny." Maggie held on to Penny's hand. "I mean it. For everything. For being with me when everything was so hard and for nudging me in the right direction when I needed a shove."

"What are best friends for?" Careful of her long slip dress, Penny stepped back and sat on the antique couch. The pale gold silk gown slid against her skin.

She ran a finger over the worn velvet of the couch. If it were refinished it might fetch a nice price in What Goes Around Comes Around, her antiques store, but it suited the old chapel the way it was. Years of wear from weddings to funerals to christenings had made this couch unique. The story behind antiques always made them more valuable in Penny's eyes.

"Well," Penny prompted, needing to lighten the mood. "Open the gift. I bet it's a ring. Probably the kind that vibrates. You know, the kind that goes on his—"

"Penny!" Maggie was too serious for her own good sometimes. Penny just smiled and shrugged. She hoped that she helped to corrupt her friend just a little.

"Just because that would be something *you'd* like for a gift…" Maggie took off the ribbon and opened the box. She drew out two diamond drop earrings. "Oh, my."

"Looks like someone is making up for lost time." Penny smiled, kicked off her heels and drew her already-aching feet under her. The devil himself had made those heels, but she wouldn't tell Maggie that.

"Brady being here now is all that matters." The light caught in the facets of the diamonds and burst into tiny dancing lights around the room. "They are so lovely."

"I'm so happy for you." And Penny meant it. If anyone deserved a happy ending, it was Maggie.

Penny wasn't made for marriage. Whenever she wanted a man, all she had to do was go out and find one. The clubs were only an hour away in Springfield. And if she just wanted to stay warm at night, Flicker, her new shaggy puppy, could help her out.

Maggie put the earrings on and turned to face Penny. "How do I look?"

"Like you are in love. Glowing. When Brady sees you, he's going to be the happiest man in the world." Maggie's bliss was contagious. It radiated from her like the brightest star. Maggie had made it through all the suffering and losing her mom.

After a moment, Maggie gave Penny a worried-momma look. "Luke made it in last night."

"Great." Penny gave Maggie a grin, even though her heart beat a little heavier. "It would look a little weird if I didn't have a best man to walk me down the aisle. Plus he's going to be part of your family soon."

"Are you sure you are okay with this?"

Penny took a deep breath and gave Maggie a reassuring look. "It was nine years ago, Maggie. Teenage puppy love. I'm sure he's over it by now. I am."

"So no drama?" Maggie raised her eyebrow.

"If there's drama, I won't be the cause of it." Penny uncurled from the couch and stood, shaking any wrinkles out of the floor-length gown. The energy levels in her body had suddenly surged and she couldn't sit anymore. Suppressing a whimper, she shoved her feet back in her shoes. She nervously checked the mirror. Her makeup hadn't smeared. Her red hair had been pulled into a tight bun, and at least one can of hair spray had plastered it into place. With the extra few inches the heels provided, she'd at least be able to look Luke Ward in the chin after all these years.

The noise level in the hallway picked up. Someone knocked on the door.

"Five minutes, ladies." The door muffled an older woman's voice beyond recognition.

"He's not seeing anyone," Maggie continued. She picked up her veil and worked the comb into her hair.

"Too bad for him, I guess." Penny held the end of the veil and straightened it to keep busy. "Seriously, Maggie, I'll be okay. Luke is here for one weekend. The worst thing that could happen is that I'll step on his foot during the bridal party dance with these fabulous heels and he'll have to bandage himself up."

"If you're sure…" Maggie didn't sound as if she believed Penny.

"I'm sure that if we don't get out there soon, the groom will think you ran away." Penny picked up the bridal bouquet and handed it to Maggie. "You worry about walking down that aisle and not about me."

Penny gave Maggie a once-over before picking up her own flowers. The last thing her friend should be worried about today was what would happen when Luke and Penny were in the same room for the first time since she had driven him away.

It was not as if they had the type of love that would last forever. Teenage love never did. First loves never did.

Luke had been heading off to college, and she'd barely earned the grades to graduate high school. If it weren't for What Goes Around Comes Around, the only work Penny would be qualified for was as either a gas station attendant or a fast-food worker. When she had inherited the quaint store along Main Street from her grandmother, it had been bleeding money, but the shop meant too much to Penny to let it fail. After her grandmother died, she had no family left to rely on. Her father had been a no-show since she was born, and her mother had ditched her years ago to continue boozing without a child in tow. But Penny was an adult now. She had managed to turn the shop around and make it a tourist attraction in their little one-stoplight town.

Through it all, she'd always had Maggie's support. Maggie and her daughter, Amber, were her family, and she wouldn't dream of making a fuss on one of the happiest days of Maggie's life. Even if that meant putting up with Brady Ward's younger brother.

The moment she stepped into the hallway, she saw him.

Luke stood about a dozen feet in front of her. The air around her crackled with energy. Dark hair, blue eyes, towering height, these were all features shared by the Ward brothers. Luke wasn't as tall as Sam, the oldest brother, but he still towered over her even in her three-inch heels. The lankiness of high school was gone, replaced by a filled-out but trim figure his tuxedo suited just fine. His dark hair curled slightly at the ends, where it touched his collar. If this were any other man, Penny would be placing bets that she would have him in her bed before the night was over.

But this was her Luke. At least he had been hers. Behind the bleachers, in the backseat of her car, in the field on a blanket looking up into a night sky that seemed to go on forever. They'd made promises neither of them were old enough to keep. Things had seemed so clear to her then. He loved her. He'd promised forever, but she knew forever was just a word. Love didn't matter. Back then it had been only a matter of time. And when—not if—he had left her, she would have been the one picking up the pieces. She straightened her shoulders and loosened the death grip on her flowers.

Plastering a smile on her face, she stepped forward.

"Penny!" Amber's voice burst out from behind Luke and the speeding golden bullet of eight-year-old energy raced toward her. "Penny! Penny! You have to meet my uncle Luke. I have two uncles now. And he's a doctor."

Penny was powerless as Amber grabbed her hand and dragged her toward Luke. Not exactly the image she'd wanted to project, but Amber didn't wait for graceful entrances.

"Amber, I've met your uncle Luke. We went to school together." Penny managed to not fall off her heels as Amber stopped in front of Luke.

"She's got quite the grip, doesn't she?" Luke smiled down at Amber as Penny tried to compose herself.

Amber spotted Maggie and took off in the direction of her mother.

"You should see her with my puppy, Flicker." Penny held her breath as Luke's gaze floated over her dress up to her face. She wasn't eighteen anymore. What if he didn't like what he saw?

Nonsense. She never let a man make her feel insecure.

Luke finally met her eyes. "I'm supposed to walk you down the aisle."

Her world was lost in a sea of blue, so rich and inviting that if she could, she would strip naked and dive into their warm depths. Warmth soaked through her body and her knees felt loose in their sockets.

She shook herself out of his spell and managed a smile that didn't feel entirely plastic. "Yes, you are."

"Or from the looks of those heels, keep you from falling on your ass?" That mischievous twinkle she'd always loved lit in his eyes.

"Oh, these little things?" Penny lifted her shoe to contemplate it.

Apparently the past was where it belonged: in the past. She smiled easier. Luke hadn't changed much since high school, but his shoulders seemed less tight. Maybe he'd finally learned to let things go. When she'd first noticed him as more than just another classmate, he'd been filled with anger and grief after the death of his parents. She knew what it was like to be left by the ones you loved. And even though his parents hadn't meant to leave, the pain he'd felt had seemed close to her own.

"Looks like we'll be spending most of the evening together," Luke said.

Penny blinked up at him as her stomach gave a little flip of joy at the remembrance of nights spent in his arms. Hot nights in the back of her beat-up Chevy. They'd laughed and forgotten about the rest of Tawnee Valley while they lost themselves in exploring each other. Fogged windows. Naked skin to naked skin. His hands and mouth had made her forget how to breathe.

"I'm the best man," he said, slowly. "And you're the maid of honor...."

"Of course." She tried to laugh it off, but it came out stilted as she tried to control the heat bubbling within her. "I'd hate to keep you from your date, though."

"I didn't bring one."

"She couldn't make it?" Penny fished just a little, knowing that if there was a *she,* Penny needed to shut down this attraction. She didn't mess with taken men.

"There isn't a she." He looked over her shoulder briefly before returning his gaze to her eyes. "What about your date? Won't it make him jealous that I'll have you in my arms most of the night?"

"If he existed, it probably would." The men she hooked up with were always free agents and never more than that. "I guess that means I'm yours tonight."

His dark eyebrow lifted as if his train of thought had just arrived at the same station. A spark of awareness raced down her spine.

"If everyone could line up," Beatrice Miller called out in her singsong voice. The kindergarten teacher helped out at the church for the wedding coordinator. She treated every wedding party like a group of five-year-olds who needed to get in line and wait patiently for their turn. Many of them had had her as a teacher, so it wasn't hard for her to rein them in.

Luke held out his elbow, and Penny hesitated for only a moment before slipping her hand over his jacketed arm. They were to be the first down the aisle.

"Mom and Dad should be here," Luke said so softly that she almost missed it.

Her fingers squeezed his arm and she leaned against him. "Yes."

As they stood by the door waiting for the procession music to begin, the crisp, clean scent of Luke wafted over her. He pulled her in tightly to his side. His warmth penetrated her silk dress. He was as solid next to her as he'd always been. Almost as much a safe haven to her as her grandmother's antiques store had been when she was young. Had he stayed in Tawnee Valley, would things have been different for them?

The doors to the chapel opened, and Penny straightened and put on her smile. This was Maggie's day. The past was gone. Only right now mattered. The entire town had turned out for the wedding. And they were all looking at her walking arm in arm with Luke Ward.

She could almost see the matchmaking gears in ole Bitsy Clemons's head turning on overload. Bitsy had brought every eligible man in Tawnee Valley to Penny's store. As if Penny would die if she didn't marry soon.

It was bad enough to be walking down the aisle with an ex, but to do so in front of everyone who had known how hot and heavy they had been…

They made it to the preacher and split ways. As Luke went to the other side of Brady, she turned and their eyes met. She saw a hint of humor and speculation in those eyes. She could definitely lose herself in him for a night or two. After all, he could only improve with age.

Amber started down the aisle and tossed wildflowers on the path before her. When she reached the front, she turned and sat in the pew next to Sam Ward.

The music changed and the doors reopened to reveal the bride. The congregation stood as she walked slowly down the aisle with a smile filled with such love that Penny couldn't stop the tears that sprang to her eyes.

As she reached the wedding party, Maggie passed her bouquet to Penny to hold and took Brady's hands.

Brady looked as if he'd just been handed the most precious gift in the world. It hit something inside of Penny, and she had to look away. Luke came into sharp focus.

Years ago, she'd thrown away what they had together, but she'd never forgotten. Every man she had been with, she compared to him, never truly letting him go. Once tomorrow came, she'd have to let him go again, but tonight was filled with potential.

Chapter Two

"Thought you were going to miss it," Sam said.

Luke raised an eyebrow but continued to stare out the truck window. "I was called to scrub in on a last-minute surgery."

Sam grunted. "Family's not that important."

If the reception had been any closer to the chapel, Luke would have walked rather than get in the truck with his oldest brother. Sam had helped raise him after their father died when Luke was fourteen. Two years later, their mother had succumbed to cancer and Brady had gone off to college, leaving only Luke and Sam.

"Of course family is important." Luke flicked a piece of lint from his tux sleeve. "Which is why I'm here today. When it matters."

Sam gave a noncommittal sound as he pulled into the parking lot of the Knights of Columbus. The hall was a standard block construction on the outside. It might not be big-city classy, but Tawnee Valley didn't offer much else in the way of reception halls.

The parking lot was already filled with trucks and cars. As soon as Luke stepped out of the truck, he could hear the music floating out of the double doors that were outlined with a pretty trellis of flowers.

"I don't know why Brady didn't just have the wedding in New York," Luke mumbled.

"Because the people in this town are as much his family as we are." Sam walked past and into the banquet room.

Luke followed him in and actually did a double take. If he hadn't just driven up to the concrete building, he would believe that he'd been dropped into a grand ballroom inside a five-star hotel. The stage had had a face-lift since the last time Luke had been here, which had to have been almost five years ago. One of his high school friends had his wedding reception here, but it had been a potluck with lots of balloons, not an elegant buffet with waiters bringing guests drinks and appetizers. The room was decorated to rival the most elegant of ballrooms, down to the artful arrangements of wildflowers on every table.

"Kind of blows your mind, doesn't it?" Penny appeared at his side.

"Definitely." Just as she did. His pulse quickened. Penny hadn't been at that wedding years ago, and they'd managed to avoid each other the few times he'd been back since their breakup. This was the first time they'd seen each other in nine years.

"Brady arranged most of it, but Maggie had the final say." Penny was every bit as attractive as he remembered, from her coppery-red hair to her brown eyes to a body with curves in all the right places to her full lips that begged for his kiss. "Come on. I'll show you the table and give you a quick walk-through of what you missed last night."

Her fingers threaded through his as she pulled him forward into the crowd. The heat of her worked its way from their entwined fingers to the center of him. Her gold dress seemed like more of a long negligee made of slightly thicker material. His fingers itched to run over her silk-covered flesh.

"The DJ is one of the best in the industry."

Luke followed her gaze to the DJ table. "Wyatt Graham?" Wyatt had graduated high school a few years after them.

Penny smiled and winked. "The local industry isn't that diverse. He'll be playing a mix of modern and oldies. We'll be required to dance together at the end of the bridal dance and for the next few dances after that."

As Luke glanced around, he noticed more familiar faces—from the waitstaff to the cooks in the opening to the kitchen. All local people, from either Tawnee Valley or the neighboring city of Owen.

"Brady could have flown the whole town to New York for what this cost."

"That wasn't the point." Penny pulled him behind a large curtain thing that gave the room its illusion of class, and leaned against the old paneled walls of the hall. The scent of musty wood overwhelmed the small space. The lighting barely filtered through the curtain. It even deadened the low roar of the crowd and the soft music playing in the background. Everyone disappeared. It was just the two of them. His imagination went wild with possibilities, but he reined them all in.

He opened his mouth.

Penny put her fingers over his lips. "Just because

you are a hotshot doc from the city doesn't mean that everything should happen in the city. Brady wanted to give the people around here a chance to be part of the wedding. It was important to both of them, so not another word about anywhere else but here."

The dim light caught and danced devilishly in her brown eyes. Her fingers were warm against his lips. They stood close together. It would take only a second to pull her into his arms and claim a kiss. He let out a breath across her fingers. Her breathing hitched, but she didn't pull away.

"Now." She sounded breathless, and his body reacted. "Do I have your promise to behave?"

The wicked glint in her eyes made her request comical.

"Do you want me to behave?" His words caressed her fingers.

He felt the tremor ripple through her. Her lips curled up in an invitation.

The music in the room suddenly changed and Penny's eyes widened. "Oh, crap, it's the entrance music."

She grabbed his hand once again and pulled him out into the open. It had been so easy to forget about the whole wedding reception happening beyond the curtain. He was half tempted to pull her back and forget about the party altogether.

Maggie and Brady walked into the hall and the crowd burst into applause.

"Brady looks happy." Luke couldn't contain that little bit of skepticism from his voice. Luke's memories of Brady were tainted with the death of his parents and the iron rule of his brother. Brady had been one of the reasons he'd finally calmed down enough to graduate high school. Penny had been the other reason.

"He should be." She leaned against his arm. "She's happy."

A wistfulness he could have imagined had entered her voice.

Luke became aware that Penny was still holding his hand while they stood watching the couple work their way through the crowd. "Are you happy?"

She gave him a mischievous smile and squeezed his hand. "I could be happier."

The suggestion was far from discreet. If it were any other time and any other woman, he might have walked away from her right then. He didn't play games. His career was his primary focus and it didn't leave time for anything else.

But tonight was his brother's wedding in his hometown, and he was standing next to the girl who had rocked his world as a teenager before she ripped his heart out and threw it back in his face. Tomorrow he'd be on a flight to St. Louis to continue his residency and Penny would return to his past, where she belonged.

"I could always tell when you were overthinking something." Penny's finger reached up and traced a line between his eyebrows. "You know that's going to form a wrinkle if you keep doing it, right?"

"So you're saying I shouldn't think?" Luke tried to read her facial expressions, but Penny had always been careful to mask what she was really feeling. He'd thought he had been behind her wall once, but he knew better now.

"Thinking is highly overrated." Penny winked at him. "We need to go to the table now. Do you think you can turn off that mega-powered brain of yours for the evening and just enjoy?"

Did she mean that he should enjoy her again? Or

was it just wishful thinking on his part? One thing was certain—he wouldn't make himself a fool for Penny this time. "I'll try."

Penny sat between Maggie and Amber, and Luke sat on the other side of Brady next to Sam at the hour-long gourmet dinner. Penny wanted to continue flirting with Luke during the meal, but it was fun talking with Amber and teasing Maggie. Her wineglass never seemed to empty and she lost track of how much she'd actually had. She felt a bit tipsy but not drunk. With her family history, she tried to be careful with alcohol.

When Maggie, Amber and Brady got up to go visit guests at their tables, Penny scooted over into Maggie's chair and leaned across Brady's.

"Having fun yet?" She batted her eyelashes at Luke in mock flirtation.

"I can say the view definitely just got better." Luke's gaze rested on her cleavage and her gaping neckline.

She didn't make any move to cover herself or even to sit up straight. "Do you have your toast ready?"

He patted his jacket. "Color-coded index cards and all."

"You really know how to get a girl's motor going." She purred and moved back to her seat. She straightened the top of her dress and winked at the elderly man sitting at the table in front of the head table. He blushed and turned away.

Penny and the town of Tawnee Valley hadn't always been on the best terms. As one of the juvenile delinquents most likely to be pregnant at sixteen and most likely to have an arrest record by the age of twenty, she'd surprised them all with the success of her store.

But that didn't mean she didn't enjoy poking at the town's notions of propriety now and then.

The wedding coordinator, Rebecca, directed Maggie and Brady over to the cake. Rebecca had performed miracles to turn this old men's club into a ballroom worthy of Maggie. Given it was the woman's first time coordinating an effort this big, she had done an amazing job. Penny was impressed with the transformation of the hall, and even the chapel had been given an overhaul.

Everyone watched Brady and Maggie cut the cake while the photographer took at least a dozen photos. When they gave each other bites, they were respectful of each other and didn't goof around as Penny would have.

The couple returned to their seats as the waitstaff brought everyone a piece of cake and poured champagne into their flutes. Down the table, Luke picked up his spoon and clinked it against his glass as he rose to standing.

"I'd like to say a few words." Luke reached into his pocket and pulled out a stack of index cards. He glanced her way slyly as he fanned through the colored cards.

Penny stifled a laugh. She'd thought he'd been joking.

"I could tell you lewd jokes or make fun of my brother for the way he used to run around the farm in his underwear and a cape when he was seven, but I won't. I could talk about the fights we three used to get into and the trouble we helped each other out of, but I won't. I could tell you about Brady's adventures overseas or his high life in New York City, but I won't." Luke set the cards on the table and his gaze went over the crowded room.

Penny found herself leaning forward to listen to

whatever he was going to say next. When Luke spoke, even back in grade school, he commanded his audience's attention. He made sure to meet everyone's eyes in the audience to make them feel included. His even tone and that deep voice kept her mesmerized. His raw emotion and honesty bonded him with the audience.

His gaze briefly met hers before settling on Brady and Maggie.

"Everyone in this room is aware of the struggles our family has had to endure. We didn't always make the right decisions, but in the end, it looks like Brady found the one thing that matters most. Someone who loves him and wants to share a life with him. A hidden treasure waiting for him to come home."

Penny could feel a thickening in her throat and blinked to hold the tears back.

"We brothers have lost so much, but Brady has finally found his family. Here's to many years of shared joy and love. To Maggie and Brady."

The crowd repeated, "To Maggie and Brady."

A pause lingered while everyone took a drink. Penny met Luke's eyes over the rim of her glass. As the crowd applauded the speech, Penny smiled at Luke before standing.

She waited for the noise to die down and then cleared her throat. "I may not be as eloquent as our doctor, but I'll give it my best shot."

She turned to Maggie. "When I was a little girl, there was one place I always knew I'd be welcome. Maggie has been my best friend, my confidante, my family for as long as I can remember. She's always been there for me and I've always tried to be there for her."

Maggie reached out, took Penny's hand and gave it a

gentle squeeze. They both had the battle scars on their hearts to prove their long-standing friendship.

"If anyone is capable of loving forever, it's Maggie, and I know I'm not the only one in the room thinking that Brady is the luckiest man alive." Still holding Maggie's hand, Penny looked at Brady. "There aren't many people I would trust with my best friend's heart, but I trust you to keep it safe and to love her until you are old and gray and need to yell at each other to be heard. I love you both and wish you happiness."

Clearing her throat, Penny blinked back the tears that had snuck up on her again. She turned to Amber. "Amber made me promise to wish you one more thing." She held up her glass and gave a grin to the rest of the hall. "To a wonderful family, and may they be blessed with a little brother or sister for Amber."

The crowd chuckled as they clinked glasses once more. Penny sank into her seat and took a drink. The DJ put on some background music and the low din of conversations grew again. Maggie and Brady were lost in their own little world. Amber had wandered off to the kids' table to be with her friends.

Suddenly Penny felt isolated. Maggie had always been the person she talked to at these types of things. Not that she needed constant attention. Lord knew she spent more than her fair share of evenings at home with no one to talk to but the dog.

She used to see Maggie everyday. But now… Brady, Maggie and Amber would be leaving to go on their two-week vacation slash honeymoon at Disney World in a few days. It would be only a few weeks, but Maggie had been preoccupied with the wedding and Brady for months now, giving Penny a lot more alone time than usual. Penny was happy for her friend, but it didn't make her miss Maggie any less.

"I think this empty chair is a better conversationalist than Sam." Luke sat in Amber's seat. His smile warmed her down to her toes.

Her heart pounded a little harder. The champagne must be going to her head because all she could do was smile at him.

"The chair has definitely improved since you arrived," she said. She could spend hours just listening to the sound of his voice. Her whole body flushed with heat and tingled in anticipation of just the slightest touch.

It was crazy. For years, she'd avoided the emotional and clung to the physical. But with Luke, it had been different. Still, that was a long time ago. They were adults now. She was more than happy to bask in the warmth of his smile for the hours they had together.

Chapter Three

"Presenting Mr. and Mrs. Ward for their first dance," the DJ announced.

Luke stood next to the dance floor with his hands in his pockets as the strains of some slow song pounded out of the speaker behind him. This was how Penny and he had started. A school dance. It had been the social hour after a football game. The student DJ was set up in the cafeteria. No fancy lights had lit the floor then. In fact, most of the lights had been turned off, making the small space feel even tighter. He'd been standing on the side with the other football players, and Penny had appeared out of nowhere in a pair of cutoffs that would have gotten her sent home from school and a T-shirt that hugged her young body.

He knew Penny Montgomery. They'd shared classes since fifth grade. In high school, she'd transformed into the kind of girl who was hard for a teenage boy to ignore. From her red hair to her smoking body to her devil-may-care attitude, she was a high school boy's fantasy.

"Dance with me." She'd smiled with her red lips and pulled him onto the dance floor before he could say anything. The music had heavy bass and a bump-and-grind rhythm.

"I don't dance," he'd managed to protest once they were in the middle of the floor.

She gave him a pout and the wicked glint in her eyes had made his pants tighten. "Don't worry. I'll show you what to do."

A touch on his shoulder brought him back to the present. Penny stood there with a smile on her lips. Her makeup was softer now, but she was just as beautiful. The slow song was about halfway through.

"Would the rest of the wedding party join in?" the DJ said over the speaker.

Luke shook off the past and held out his hand to Penny. She slipped her hand in his and followed his lead out to the dance floor. She moved into his arms like a missing puzzle piece.

Sam and Amber followed them onto the dance floor, drawing everyone's attention. Amber put her feet on top of Sam's and he held her hands. It was strange watching Sam with a child. As Luke's pseudo-parent, Sam had been distant but controlling. Now he seemed perfectly at ease talking with his niece, even if he didn't smile.

Luke's attention returned to the woman he held in his arms for the first time in almost a decade.

"Looks like someone's been practicing," she said. That flirtatious tilt was back in Penny's smile.

"I try to maintain appearances."

"I'm sure you have your admirers." A teasing glint

in her eyes and a soft smile on her lips betrayed nothing of what she really felt, but that was Penny.

"I do love compliments." He led them toward a
darker area of the dance floor as other couples joined in.

"I bet you do."

Years ago, that first night, when the music had
slowed down she'd moved into his arms and her breasts
had pressed against his chest, her body close to his.
Hormones had flooded him, making it hard to think…
Why was he getting wrapped up in the past?

His fingers tightened into the softness of Penny's
waist.

She closed the slight gap between them and whispered, "Stop thinking, Luke."

"Why aren't you with someone, Penny?"

"I'm with you right now." Her eyes may never reveal
her inner thoughts, but he noticed a slight hesitance in
her words. Her body pressed slightly closer until there
was no more than a whisper between them.

"You know what I mean." Luke tried to hold on to
the thoughts in his head as his body tried to make them
all vanish. Her light perfume smelled like spring flowers, the scent's innocence at odds with the seductive
woman. It surrounded him, begging him to bend down
and breathe in. To touch the warmth of her neck with
his lips.

"Who should I be with? The town drunk, the divorcé
with the ex from hell—"

"Sam."

She stopped dancing and her lips drew tight. "Sam?"

Penny was in his arms and he wasn't about to back
off. Not when her soft curves filled in his rough patches.
This was important. He didn't want to step in between

his brother and anyone, even if that anyone had been the only girl Luke had ever given his heart to.

"You two were pretty tight last time I saw you." The last time he'd seen Penny, at his graduation party, she'd been kissing Sam.

She pushed against his chest, but he didn't budge. Her eyes flashed up at him. Was that hurt? It had been there for a moment, but it was gone so fast he must have imagined it. It felt as if she was going to push again, but instead she softened. The walls closed in her eyes.

"Sam never meant anything to me." She placed her hands back on his shoulders. "We never had more than a kiss. I'm surprised he didn't tell you."

"Why would he?" Some of the tension released from his grip. Luke's brain was quickly losing the battle with his body's needs. It shouldn't matter why she kissed Sam or even that she did. It had been years ago. It had stopped him from making a major mistake.

Sure it had hurt then, but he'd brought it up now to draw out the woman he'd known from this seductress before him.

She shrugged. "You don't really want to talk about Sam, do you, Luke?"

He didn't know what he was trying to prove. He looked around the dance floor. Now wasn't the time to rehash the past. No time would be the right time. "No."

"How about a drink?" she said. Her gaze flicked over his face.

"A couple of glasses of wine between old friends? Why not. Wait here."

Penny's heart pounded as she sank into a chair and watched Luke walk away. Her knees had barely held her up. Without Luke's arms around her, she would have been down on the ground. She watched him move through the crowd.

Sam had been a means to an end. She'd hated herself for using him, but it had done exactly what she needed it to. Luke had to leave for college without her.

As the DJ cued up some fast dance music, Penny took a deep breath. Tonight had turned out perfectly for Brady and Maggie. They were dancing with Amber in the circle of people on the dance floor.

If her knees recovered, she might go join them. A glass of wine appeared over her shoulder and Luke's breath teased the hairs on the back of her neck. "I had to turn down a lot of eligible ladies to get back here."

Glancing over at the bar, she took the wineglass and felt him sit in the chair behind hers. All of her cells were attuned to whatever frequency Luke gave off. At the bar stood a gathering of white-haired women all giving Luke come-hither looks and finger waves.

Penny choked back a laugh. She tried her hardest to look serious when she turned to Luke. "I hope you let them down easy. It's just as hard to find a man at their age as mine."

Leaning in so he could speak in her ear and be heard over the music, Luke's cheek rubbed against hers, sending a wave of heat through her. "I always try to be gentle."

"I'm sure you do." She could feel his cheek lift in a grin. A shiver rippled down her back.

He moved back until they were eye to eye. "They were actually encouraging me to hit on the wedding coordinator."

Penny glanced over at Rebecca in her peach suit. She was a few years younger than Penny and looked as if the pressure of this wedding was about to make her explode.

"I suppose you could go for Rebecca…." Penny put on a pretend thoughtful look.

The music changed to a slow song again. "Come on. You can tell me all about what that look means on the dance floor."

Luke pulled her out of the chair and guided her into his arms. She'd given up on love songs when Luke left, preferring the rawness of modern rock. Slow songs messed with her brain and made her think about things she couldn't have.

"So are we for or against chatting up the wedding coordinator?" Luke raised his eyebrow as he looked down at Penny.

"I think she'd have an aneurysm if 'we' approached her." Penny mocked Luke's look.

Luke laughed. "Fair enough. Besides, I'm only here until tomorrow. Wouldn't be fair to get anyone's hopes up."

"No, you wouldn't want to do that."

He pressed his hand into the small of her back and she allowed herself to move closer to him. To breathe in his scent. To feel the heat of his body against hers. The song didn't matter as long as it didn't stop.

"Besides—" he leaned down as if he had a secret to whisper in her ear "—I always heard that the best man was supposed to hook up with the maid of honor."

Penny's breathing hitched as she met his eyes. "I think it's actually a written law somewhere that if both parties are single, it's required."

"So we'd be in a lot of trouble if we didn't at least attempt to…" He wiggled his eyebrows.

"Heaps of trouble." Her heart beat hard against her chest as she tried to keep a teasing tone.

"We wouldn't want that." Luke gave her a cocky

smile. "But then you were never the type to follow rules."

"I'll have you know I'm one of the upstanding citizens in Tawnee Valley now."

"Really?" His sarcastic tone made her laugh.

"I'm a valued member of the Chamber of Commerce. My shop brings in tons of tourists."

"I guess that nails it, then." He made a serious face even though his eyes were twinkling. Still dancing, he led her to the side of the dance floor. "Rules are rules, after all."

She swallowed as liquid heat flooded her system. Her fingers locked around the back of his neck. "I suppose after the reception…"

The heat in his blue eyes made her breath catch. He didn't have to say he wanted her. It was there and it scorched her through to her soul. She didn't want to wait. It had been too long since she'd held him, since her skin had brushed against his.

His smile grew cocky. "Why wait?"

Penny glanced around them. The music had shifted to a fast song again. Most everyone was on the dance floor. Amber was dancing with her parents. Sam was brooding in a corner with a glass of liquor. The older folks were on the other side of the dance floor gathered around a few tables. It looked as if they were shouting to talk above the music.

His hand closed firmly around hers and she met his eyes. Apparently they'd reached the same conclusion. No one would miss them if they ducked out at this moment. She doubted anyone would even think anything of it if they did disappear.

Luke started backing up, pulling her with him. Giddiness welled inside her, the same feeling she used to get in high school when Luke would pick her up for a date. Anticipation mixed with the knowledge that no one would know what they were doing. Something hidden that was hers alone.

"You know, I'm not this type of guy." He stopped and pulled her hard until she stumbled into his chest. His teasing smile made her heart skip a beat. "I usually require dinner and wine first."

She smiled up at him. "Good thing we came to a wedding, then. Dinner, check. Wine, check."

"I wouldn't want you to think less of me." He was joking around, but her heart wouldn't let her say something flippant. It demanded she let him know this much.

"Nothing would make me think less of you."

He glanced over her shoulder toward the rest of the party as they approached the exit. "Where should we go?"

When he turned back to her, she forgot to breathe, let alone think. She knew that in Luke's eyes, they were equals, but she'd always known she wasn't as good as he was. During sex was the only time she felt like his match.

"Follow me." She led him past the curtain and into the darkness behind it. The closet door opened easily and she slid in with Luke behind her.

"Classy," Luke muttered. The door closed and the small space seemed to close in on them. Even the music was muffled beyond recognition. The smell of lemon cleaner tinged the air.

"If you'd rather go out in the parking lot and risk causing Bitsy heart palpitations when she sees me straddling you in your brother's truck—"

"Stop thinking, Penny." In the darkness, he moved closer until she felt his whole body pressed against hers.

Her breath quickened as she waited. For his next move. For his touch. For his kiss.

She felt the brush of his arm next to her and caught her breath. The click of the lock could barely be heard over the sound of their breaths. The warm, clean scent of Luke filled her.

"You don't have to do this." Luke's whispered words caressed her earlobe. "Just because we're here at a wedding doesn't mean we have to have sex."

"Are you trying to give *me* an out, Luke Ward?" She laughed, releasing some of the tension that had been welling within her. "I must be pretty darned good if you think this is all your idea."

He chuckled and his knuckles brushed over her jaw, ending her own laughter. "I don't want you to think I only want sex."

"What else would you want?" She didn't bother trying to hide the breathiness of her voice.

His forehead pressed against hers and his hands ran up and down her arms. "I don't know."

Her heart beat with his quickened breath. Once, twice, three times.

She slid off her heels and lifted onto her toes. Pressing a kiss to his jaw, she could feel his heart beat in time with hers against her palm. "I want you."

His lips closed over hers. Sparks rippled through her as he pulled her in close. Relief spiraled out of her heart even as her pulse quickened. Her memories of his kisses collapsed under the weight of this one. It wasn't the technique that had her clutching at his dress shirt—though the technique was definitely good. It was the man.

In an instant, she knew if it were ten years from now,

even a hundred, and Luke kissed her, it would still feel like this. Explosive, powerful, soul shattering.

Desire pulsed within her, and that little piece of her that would always belong to Luke throbbed with satisfaction. He was kissing her as if they had only moments to live. Maybe they did. Maybe she felt alive only when Luke was here. Kissing her.

His hands clutched at the fabric around her hips, slowly easing the silky material up her calves and over her thighs. It was as if the silk were his fingers trailing ever higher, stealing her breath.

She unclenched her fingers and started undoing the buttons of his shirt. The need to feel his skin against hers was overwhelming. His warmth beckoned beneath the fabric. The cool air caressed her legs as her dress slipped up over her hips. The crisp fabric of his tux pants brushed against her skin.

Pulling his shirt free of his pants, she opened it. His fingers brushed under the edge of her panties at her hips. She leaned back against the door as his lips left her mouth and trailed kisses along her jaw.

The warmth of his chest beckoned. She ran her fingers over the muscles, making a mental picture in the dark. Memorizing the contours. As her hand slid down his abs, he sucked in his breath and nipped at her neck.

Power coursed through her veins as she eased down his zipper and brushed the hardness underneath. He grabbed her hands and pushed them against the door, reclaiming her mouth.

The silk dress rushed down her thighs, but caught as his knee moved between her legs. The door and Luke had her captured, unable to escape. Not that she wanted freedom. If she could, she would spend eternity in this little closet with Luke.

This wasn't like a one-night stand or even a booty call. Luke wouldn't fill just her need for an orgasm. She craved relief, but she didn't want this to end.

She'd made a mistake.

Having Luke one more time wouldn't fulfill some need for closure. The sound of his pants dropping filled the space between them.

Even knowing this was a mistake, she wanted him. Even though it would only widen the hole he'd left behind. Even as her body hummed from his touch, she wanted to cry.

She'd take what she could from him and he'd leave. That would be the end of it. She'd survived before and she'd survive this time.

"Are you okay?" He kissed her next to her ear as his fingers teased the edge of her underwear.

She sucked in a breath as his hand slipped under the fabric and touched her skin. Wrapping her hands behind his head, she pulled his mouth to hers. She was beyond being okay. She needed to shut down her brain and feel. Brand him the way he branded her.

He slid off her underwear. Her dress remained bunched up around her waist. His bare skin brushed against hers. Rough against soft. She heard him open a condom packet.

After a moment, his hands returned to her hips and his mouth returned to hers. He lifted her against the door and she wrapped her legs around his waist. In the darkness all she could do was feel. The real world was far away. The fact that they were in a closet at a wedding didn't matter. All that mattered was that he was with her now.

"Say my name," he whispered against her ear. The darkness engulfed them. They could only feel and hear.

But she knew it meant more to him. It was his way of claiming her, of making sure she knew it was him and not any number of guys.

She wanted to please him, needed him to know that it was only him. That it had always been only him.

"Luke." Her world came unhinged as he entered her slowly. His hands held her hips. The tears she'd been holding back pressed forward. She repeated his name and muttered words she couldn't be held accountable for as he moved within her, the only thing she could allow herself from him.

The tears edged over her eyes and trailed down her cheeks as her body rejoiced. It felt like coming home and like nothing she'd ever felt before. Dangerous and tempting. Something she never should have messed with. He lifted her higher and higher until she fell over the edge into bliss. He joined her with her name on his lips.

She choked back a sob and held him tighter, never wanting to let go.

Chapter Four

Luke fought to steady his breathing in the dark room. Penny fit against his body perfectly. He wanted to continue to hold her, but the noise of the party beyond the door told him that they needed to get back. Her breath shuddered in and out. Lowering her gently to the floor, he stepped back. In the dark he couldn't see her, but it sounded as if she was crying. "Did I hurt you?"

"No."

Suddenly the dark that had wrapped them in an intimate fog pissed him off. He could tell she was lying but couldn't prove it.

"Something's wrong." Luke felt the wall next to the door for a light switch.

"Nothing's wrong." She reached past him and the light blinked on. For a moment he was blind as his eyes adjusted to the brightness.

Penny had bent down and retrieved her underwear. "We need to get back out there."

"Nothing's wrong, my ass." Luke pulled up his boxers and pants.

"What do you want me to say?" She turned her back to him as she fixed her clothing. "It was fantastic, wonderful, the best thing ever."

"What's gotten into you?" The lightness in his chest grew heavy. Trying to recapture the mood, he dropped a kiss on the nape of her neck.

Her shoulders tensed but then relaxed. When she turned around, the plastic smile was in place. He closed his eyes for a moment and took a deep breath. Whatever had made her upset, she wasn't going to tell him.

"I'm fine. Really. We just need to get back." Her flirtatious smile returned. "I had a really good time."

She moved to open the door, but he grabbed the knob to hold it closed.

"Fine? You are far from fine. You can act all you want for the revolving door of men you have, but I know you." The anger raging within was tempered by the orgasm he'd just had. After he'd left all those years ago, he'd heard about her escapades from classmates and folks around town. They had acted as if he should step in and do something. He didn't tell them that he'd heard the rumors of her with other guys the entire time they'd dated.

She didn't even bristle. She reached up to fix his collar as if they were discussing the weather. "Is that what you are worried about? That I'm comparing you to other lovers?"

"What I'm worried about is the fact that you don't seem to feel anything anymore." Luke brushed her hair away from her face. "Does anything matter to you?"

Her smile didn't show even a hint of anger, which just made him more determined to break through that wall. To what end? He didn't know.

"You're leaving tomorrow?" Her brown eyes lifted to his.

He nodded, not really wanting to be reminded of that at this moment.

"Let's go out to the party and afterward…" She held on to his shoulders as she slipped her feet into her shoes.

His imagination could do a lot of things with *afterward*.

She kissed his jaw. "Afterward."

The background noise changed. It had been so subtle he hadn't even noticed the music and laughing beyond the door, but the sudden lack of it gained his attention. He thought he heard someone call his name.

"Something's happening." Luke opened the door and found his way out from behind the curtain. The overhead lights were on and everyone was hovering near the dance floor.

Luke's heart pounded against his chest as he saw someone lying on the floor beyond the crowd. His training kicked in as he rushed forward.

Breaking through the crowd, he froze when he saw Sam unconscious on the ground, his face ashen. Luke's world lurched. "What happened?"

"He just fell over," an old man who looked familiar said.

"Everyone back up and give him some space," Luke ordered. "Has anyone called 911?"

"Yes. The ambulance is on the way."

Luke checked Sam's pulse. He was still breathing, but his pulse was faint. "Bring over a chair."

Luke pulled Sam's bow tie off and unbuttoned his

collar. When Amber dragged over a chair, Luke lifted Sam's feet up onto the seat.

"Where are Brady and Maggie?" Luke asked the nearest woman.

"They just left."

"Is he going to be okay?" Tears ran freely down Amber's cheeks. Penny kneeled next to Amber and held out her arms. Amber collapsed against her but kept her big blue eyes on Luke and Sam.

"We need to get him checked at the hospital." Luke met Penny's eyes and saw the worry there.

He tried not to think about it as he worked on evaluating Sam's condition.

"The ambulance is here," someone said.

The paramedics came in and Luke gave them a rundown of what he knew, which wasn't much. Sam had fainted and hadn't regained consciousness.

"Should I call Brady and Maggie?" Penny asked as Luke stepped out of the way to let the paramedics work.

"Not yet." Luke ran a hand over his face. "They just left for their wedding night, and we have nothing to tell them. They'd just worry or, worse, spend their wedding night in the hospital waiting room."

She nodded, still holding on to Amber. "Maybe I should take Amber home."

"No." Amber shook her head. "I'm going with Uncle Sam."

"It's late. We can go wait at my house with Flicker, and your uncle Luke will call with any news." Penny's gaze met Luke's, looking for his support.

He nodded, but that wasn't enough for Amber.

"I'm supposed to stay with Uncle Sam tonight," Amber said. If Luke knew anything about his family, it was that stubbornness definitely ran in it. But he had only just met his niece.

"What if—" Penny looked up at Luke "—we go to the hospital and see that Uncle Sam is taken care of, then you and I will go get Flicker and drive out to check on the farm?"

Luke nodded in agreement. What else could he do until he knew what was going on with Sam?

"I wanna ride in the ambulance." Amber turned her stubborn little chin up at Luke.

"No," Penny said, her voice more firm than he'd ever heard it before. "You ride with me or the deal is off, kiddo."

"Okay." Amber pouted but went to grab her flowers and sweater from their table.

"Did you want to ride with us or with the ambulance?" Penny's presence actually calmed his racing heart for a moment.

"I'll drive Sam's truck and meet you there." Luke watched as the paramedics wheeled Sam out the door. He felt lost, as if he could have prevented whatever was happening.

Penny wrapped her arms around him in a hug that had nothing to do with sex. "He'll be all right."

He returned her hug and breathed in her floral scent. The knot in his stomach loosened slightly.

She released him before he wanted to let go, but things had to get done. "We'll be there in a few minutes. I'm going to talk to the wedding coordinator and make sure everything is taken care of before we head to the hospital."

Amber came back over with tears in her big blue eyes. "Can I ride with Uncle Luke? Please?"

Penny gave him a questioning look, leaving it up to

him. He looked around at the people waiting and the chaos beyond. It might take Penny a half hour or more to finish up here and Amber would be left sitting alone. He remembered how that felt when his father had been rushed to the hospital. No one had taken the time to tell him what was happening. He was just left waiting.

Luke held out his hand to Amber. "Sure. Let's go."

An hour later, Luke sat in the waiting room of the hospital in Owen with his niece fast asleep against his side. Sam had woken during the ambulance ride and had been cranky as ever. When he arrived at the hospital, the doctor ordered several tests to make sure he hadn't had a heart attack or wasn't on the verge of having one. The doctor had insisted Luke go to the waiting area since Sam didn't look to be in any eminent danger.

A flicker of gold caught Luke's attention. He lifted his head in the direction of the hallway. Penny sauntered toward him with her heels in one hand and a soft smile on her lips. It had been only an hour or so since he'd held her in his arms, but it felt as if an eternity had passed.

Careful not to wake Amber, she sat gently on his other side and whispered, "How's Sam?"

Luke took a deep breath and released it. "No word yet. Apparently a few months ago, he had an X-ray that showed an enlarged heart, but he skipped his follow-up with the cardiologist. The fainting could mean a number of things, from cardiomyopathy to hypothyroidism to hemo—"

Penny took his hand between hers. "Lots of doctor mumbo jumbo. Is he going to be okay?"

"I hope so." He ran his other hand through his hair. Their family history of heart disease was the reason Luke had gone to med school and why he'd specialized in cardiology. If Luke had known at fourteen what he knew now, maybe he could have prevented the heart attack that killed his father. The warning signs had all been there. No one had pushed Dad to get checked out. Not that his father could have been pushed. A trait Sam inherited.

"I guess I should take Amber home and get her into bed." Penny didn't move and he felt her eyes on him. "Unless you want me to stay."

Luke didn't know what he wanted. Earlier it had been easy to just pull Penny into his arms and forget the past and future. He would definitely prefer to argue more with Penny instead of sitting in a waiting room with months-old magazines and a news channel on a muted TV. If his niece weren't here, he might even flirt, if only for the distraction.

As if sensing his hesitation, Penny leaned forward to look around him at Amber. "If I wake Amber now, she'll be a bear to get back to sleep. Why don't I just keep you company while we wait to hear about Sam?"

"Why are you being like this?" Luke stared at the television in the corner. There was no reason for Penny to be here for him now. Not even after what happened in the closet. They weren't anything more than exes thrown together at a wedding. She didn't have to be nice to him.

She settled next to him, pulling her feet up under her and leaning her head against his shoulder. "Being like what?"

He looked down at the top of her auburn head. "It doesn't matter."

She shrugged. "When should we call Maggie and Brady?" A yawn followed as she squirmed herself into a more comfortable spot.

"It's late. We'll wait until morning and give them a call. No reason to disrupt their wedding night. As long as Sam remains stable, there's nothing they could do but worry anyway." Sam was only thirty and relatively healthy, but fainting was serious…especially with an unknown heart condition. Luke needed to get up and do something, but he couldn't without disturbing Amber. His leg started to bounce.

Penny kept hold of his hand in her lap. He should ask to look over Sam's chart and figure out if they were doing all the necessary testing. EKG, echocardiogram, CBC. Maybe he should talk to the doctor about a transfer to the nearest medical school hospital. He wondered if they could Life Flight him to his hospital in St. Louis.

"I hear you got into one of the better programs for med school," Penny said.

"What?" He pulled his gaze from the doors the doctor had vanished behind recently.

"Med school. Good program?" Penny repeated and looked up at him.

"Yeah. It took a lot of cramming, but I got the grades to get in." If he could figure out a way to slide out from under Amber without waking her, he would go through those doors that said "Authorized Personnel Only." Surely they missed something on the chart. Most hospitals generally had rules against working on family. But they probably didn't have a cardiologist on staff.

"I was glad to graduate high school with a C average," Penny scoffed. "You always were the smarter of the two of us."

"That's not true. You were just a misguided youth." He smiled at the memory.

"Remember when we were studying for my final

in Geometry? If it hadn't been for you, I wouldn't still have the useless phrase SOH CAH TOA in my head."

Luke chuckled. "Do you even remember what it means?"

Penny screwed up her nose. "Of course not. If it had been useful, then I definitely would have remembered it. I bet I haven't used half of what they forced us to learn in high school."

"You probably use more than you think." Luke sank farther into his chair. His legs relaxed out in front of him. "If we'd been together longer, I bet you would have received straight As."

"You definitely made studying fun." She rubbed her thumb across the back of his hand. "Do you remember that one night we walked all the way to Owen to The Morning Rooster to have breakfast at 2:00 a.m.?"

"I remember heading back and having to carry you piggyback half the way."

"I didn't know we were going to walk eight miles each way when I decided on my shoe choice for the evening. Most nights I didn't even need my shoes."

"I remember talking about everything that night. Philosophy, love, family, sex, shoes." He squeezed her hand. "We were quite the rebels."

"More like trendsetters. Apparently it's a new dare among the kids in Tawnee Valley. How far are you willing to walk to breakfast?"

Luke laughed. "Not like there was much else to do on Saturday nights. Especially when Sam would take away my car privileges."

"And my car was in the shop. You know, I kept that old beater until it finally coughed its final gas fumes into the air about five years ago."

"I'm surprised it made it that long." This was the part

of Penny he'd missed the most. The quiet times when it was just the two of them talking. That piece of her that only he got to see.

The doors swung open. Dr. Sanchez came into the waiting area and walked their way. "Don't get up."

Luke had automatically started to rise without thinking about Amber and Penny leaning on him. She smiled down at the three of them. Penny released his hand and he missed her warmth.

"So far the test results have been promising. It doesn't look like he suffered from cardiac arrest, but we can't rule out a future one. We'd like to keep him overnight for observation."

Luke breathed out as if he'd been holding his breath for days. No cardiac arrest was good, but Sam wasn't out of the woods yet. "What's the plan once he's released?"

"Until we have a few more test results, we won't know for sure the type and extent of damage. I can't give you any more information until tomorrow."

"But he's going to be okay?" Penny asked, straightening in the chair.

"We'll know more tomorrow." Dr. Sanchez smiled that doctor smile Luke was all too familiar with. The one that said we don't know all that much and all we can do is hope for the best. "For tonight, I suggest you go home and get a good night's sleep. We've already given Mr. Ward something to help him sleep."

"Thank you," Luke said. Because of privacy laws, the doctor wouldn't tell Luke much more, so he didn't push. Besides, until the tests were completed, the doctor wouldn't know any more than he did.

Dr. Sanchez disappeared behind the doors again.

"Why don't I drive us all out to the farm?" Penny

stretched like a cat. "It's closer to the hospital and Amber won't pitch a fit if she wakes up there. I asked Bitsy to look in on my dog when she left the reception."

Luke hesitated. It felt odd to invite Penny back to Sam's house. "It's not that I don't appreciate the offer—"

"I wasn't doing it just for you." She stood and looked down her nose at him. "Maggie is family to me. That makes Brady family and Sam by extension. I need to take care of Amber and make sure things go smoothly so those two can take their daughter to Disney World on their honeymoon and make me more babies to take care of. I'm tired and I just want to crash and be there when Amber and Maggie need me in the morning."

Luke stood and picked up Amber. Thinking of Penny with babies did something strange to his heart. "I just didn't want you to think that I needed you—"

"Trust me. I know you don't need me." He saw a flash of hurt in Penny's eyes. "Maggie and Amber need me."

"I'm sorry, Penny. I didn't mean…" Oh, hell, what did he mean? If it meant avoiding a fight and not disappointing Amber, who was he to care whether they stayed here or went to the farm? They could work out the details when they arrived. Right now, he just wanted to look at something besides these four walls. "Look, we're both tired. Why don't *I* drive us out to the farm and we'll work on it from there? It doesn't look like I'll be flying out tomorrow."

"If you are talking about staying for Sam, maybe I can help."

Help? She was the reason he hadn't been out there to help Sam in the first place. His brother might have been showing signs that he could have picked up on if he hadn't been too busy making eyes at the pretty woman in front of him. "He's my family. For now, let's go home."

"He'll be okay." Penny rested her hand above his heart.

Penny's touch comforted him in a way he'd almost forgotten. For a long moment, he searched her eyes. With Sam's condition unknown, Luke couldn't just leave. Depending on what was wrong, he might need surgery or just bed rest. His mind shuffled through all the possible diagnoses, but he didn't have the chart to see what they'd uncovered when they'd examined him today. He trusted the doctor to make the right call regarding Sam's treatment.

Regardless, his brother might be here longer than a night. What happened after tonight with Penny? They hadn't promised more than tonight because that wasn't an option. Maybe it still wasn't an option. He didn't know Penny that well anymore, but from what he heard she rarely made a habit of any man.

He needed to get out of his head. There was plenty to worry about tomorrow. First he had to get through tonight. "Let's go."

Chapter Five

Penny shut the door of the bedroom. Amber had taken very little coaxing to fall back to sleep in Brady's old bedroom. Reassuring her that Sam would be okay and they'd see him in the morning was all it had taken. The old wooden stairs creaked under her feet as she returned to the first floor. It was past two in the morning, the lights were all still on and she didn't feel tired at all.

The sound of a chair scraping across the linoleum in the kitchen drew her that way. She stopped in the doorway and leaned against the doorjamb. Luke sat at the kitchen table, his head in his hands. If she had stayed with him after high school, would things have turned out differently? Would he have made it through med school with her dragging him down? Where would she have been when he left her? Stuck in some city where she wouldn't know a soul and Maggie would have been here all alone dealing with her mother's illness and raising Amber.

She could play the what-if game, but she had decided a long time ago to live in the present. And presently, the weight of the world was on Luke's shoulders. He'd always taken on too much. All she'd ever wanted to do was take some of that weight off him. In high school, it had been easy. Nothing takes a man's mind off his problems like sex. Now they were adults with a complicated history. She had no idea of the problems he was facing in his day-to-day life, but Sam's collapse was one more thing to deal with.

Even though it had been years since they'd been together as a couple, she'd known at the hospital that he needed her to be there with him. To keep him out of his head.

"Hey," she said and shoved off the wall to join him in the kitchen.

He lifted his head and gave her a weary smile. "Hey."

"Not exactly how I thought this night would end." She flashed him a smile and leaned against the counter, putting one bare foot on top of the other. She'd ditched her killer high heels next to the door as soon as they'd walked in. They looked a little obscene next to the work boots and sneakers stacked there.

Her feet felt only half as weary as Luke looked. She wanted to go over and pull him into her arms and just hold him, but she needed to let him dictate what he needed. Whether it was just to talk or...

He rubbed his hand over his hair. "You want some coffee?"

"Nah, I should sleep at some point tonight, so I can wake up when Amber gets up." A knot formed in her stomach. He probably thought she was pushing for him to invite her to sleep with him. For once she felt awkward. This was one of those situations she avoided for just this reason. She didn't sleep over and she didn't let anyone near her bed. She was all for sex, but cuddling wasn't her style.

He started to rise from his chair. "I can set up the guest bed—"

"Is that really necessary?" She put on her best brazen-it-out smile. Typically she didn't "sleep" with anyone except her puppy, but the last thing Luke needed to do tonight was worry about making her comfortable in his family home. She'd be fine whether he wanted her in his bed or on the couch. "I can crash wherever."

When she shrugged so that he would know it wasn't a big deal, the strap from her gown slid down her arm, drawing Luke's gaze. She felt it like a physical caress. The air in the room was suddenly charged.

"You always liked to finish what you started." His gaze met hers and his eyes flamed with desire.

Her body responded with all the repressed heat she'd sidelined since their closet interlude. Her body always would react to his. But she didn't want to push him, not with everything else weighing on his mind. "You know me. I'm always game. But I leave the decision up to you. I know you have a lot on your mind right now—"

"I'd rather not think at all." Luke crossed the kitchen floor and pulled her into his arms. Her toes brushed against the warm, soft fabric of his socks. "I'd rather forget everything outside of these walls for the rest of the night. Stop my mind from circling around what I'll need to do to be able to stay here with Sam. Stop from worrying that he might not be getting sufficient care. Stop trying to figure out—"

"Just stop," she whispered and drew his head down to hers. "I won't ask you for anything."

"I know," he said before claiming her mouth.

The creak of the bed woke Luke from a deep sleep. He automatically reached for his phone on the nightstand but hit only air where his nightstand should be. He blinked into the darkness and squinted at the dim light coming through the window. Instead of city lights, he saw the moon lighting up the fields rolling into the distance. The crops swayed slightly in the breeze.

The night came rushing back to him. The wedding. Sam's collapse. Inviting Penny into his bed. A shadow moved in front of the window.

"What are you doing?" Luke sat up and rubbed his face.

She flinched and turned around to face him. He couldn't see her features, but his eyes were quickly adjusting to the darkness. Her light skin glowed in the moonlight that managed to sneak through the curtains. Standing only in her underwear, she held the rest of her dress at her waist like a shield in front of her. "I was… going to get a drink of water. Do you want some?"

"No, I don't want some water."

"More for me, then." She started to move away.

"Enough bull. What is really going on, Penny?"

She glanced at the door to the hallway and then back to the side of the bed that was still warm from her body. "I just thought…" She shrugged.

"That there isn't enough room? I snore too loudly?" He shifted off the bed and flicked on the lamp, casting the room in soft light.

She blinked but didn't move to cover herself. "What does it matter?"

"Just get back into bed, Penny. I swear we'll only sleep."

"Isn't it the woman's job to be needy and clingy?"

"Far be it from me to stop you." He stepped away from the bed and held his hand out. "I just thought you might want to be comfortable for the night. The last thing I'd want to do is make you feel needed."

Penny's shoulders pushed back and her chin tipped up. "Contrary to popular belief, a woman does not need a man to need her to feel complete."

Though her words and actions were angry, saying them nearly naked was having the opposite effect on his body. "I made you feel complete at least three times if my count is correct."

She threw her dress at him. He caught it and dropped it to the floor.

He strode across the room and grabbed her elbows, pulling her flush against his chest. "Unless you plan to traipse around the farmhouse in your underwear." At the devilish glint in her eyes, he added, "Remembering that my niece could wake up at any moment, I suggest you come back to bed."

Her body was tense against his and fire crackled in her eyes. "Maybe I don't want to sleep with you."

His hands rubbed her back. "If you don't want to sleep with me, I'm sure I could be convinced to stay awake."

Apparently he was starting to speak her language because she softened. Her curves molded into his and the heat that had pooled in his stomach flooded his system. "I've never been good at sleepovers."

"I doubt there are many people who would accuse you of being good at all." He lifted her into his arms. Penny was a puzzle. One he would be better off not trying to solve. One he should be pushing away instead of carrying back to his bed.

He lowered her onto the mattress, never releasing his hold on her body.

"Good is overrated." Penny pulled him down to her. "When has being good ever gotten you what you wanted?"

At one point, the thing he'd wanted most had been her. He'd been willing to do anything to keep her, except share her with anyone else. He lowered his head to hers. "Being good has gotten me nothing."

Chapter Six

Waiting rooms weren't nearly as bad as sitting in a patient's room, especially when the patient was Sam. Luke had taken the recliner, whereas Amber had chosen to sit at the end of Sam's bed. Apparently Sam was confident that he wasn't staying there because he'd been dressed in his tux, minus the jacket and tie, and ready to go as soon as they'd come in. When Luke had given Sam a bag with some of his clothes from home, he'd grunted a thank-you and immediately changed.

"I made sure to give the baby calves their bottles." Amber had been listing all the chores she'd insisted on helping with this morning. "I'll walk the fences this afternoon to make sure there aren't any breaks."

"I knew I could count on you." Sam smiled at his niece, if you could call the slight curve to his lips a smile.

Luke still couldn't understand Amber's loyal devotion to hardheaded Sam. This morning at the breakfast table, she'd run off a list of all the chores that she did when she stayed at the farm. While Luke had been amused with the list, he'd barely been able to keep his eyes from the woman who had kept him up all night.

Penny had moved around the kitchen with ease, as if she made breakfast there frequently. For all he knew she did. She had said she and Sam had had nothing more than that kiss years ago, but how could he believe a word that slipped past those wicked lips?

Wearing one of his T-shirts and not a whole lot more, she'd slipped out of his room. He'd assumed she'd join him after using the bathroom, but when he woke a few hours later from little feet creaking down the stairs, Penny was not in his bed.

He'd found her on the couch with an afghan pulled over her, fast asleep.

"Can I name the new piglets? Please?" Amber brought his attention back to the present. They were waiting for the doctor to talk to them and discharge Sam. Penny had excused herself as soon as they got to the hospital to go check on her puppy and to change out of Luke's oversize T-shirt and sweats.

"We can just call them Pork Chop, Ham and Bacon." Sam rested against the elevated back of the hospital bed. Luke couldn't remember the last time he'd heard Sam tease someone. Maybe when Luke had been Amber's age. Before Dad… Before Mom…

"That's not very nice, Uncle Sam." Amber gave him a look that reminded Luke of their mother when she'd scolded them even though she wanted to laugh at their antics. Sam just chuckled lightly, drawing Luke's questioning gaze to him. Sam shrugged.

"When am I getting out of this place?" Sam looked

toward the door as if willing the doctor to appear with his release instructions.

"I'm sure the staff is just as anxious for you to go," Luke said before standing. "I'm going to go find a cup of coffee. Do you want anything?" He looked at Amber.

She turned her bright blue eyes up to him and shook her head no. "I'm going to take care of Uncle Sam."

He believed her. He didn't know why she was so attached, but somehow Sam had become her hero. Or maybe Amber would be his savior. Either way, Sam must have done at least one good deed in his life to deserve her devotion.

The hallway was bustling with energy. Nurses darted in and out of rooms. The high-school-aged candy stripers were unloading the breakfast trays. The various beeping and swishing sounds of equipment blended into a discordant symphony. The smell of antiseptics filled his nose. It invigorated him. Hospitals had been his home for the past few years.

He wasn't used to being a visitor, though. Instead of part of the natural flow, he felt as if he was in the way as he walked to the coffee machine in the waiting area. As his coffee finished brewing, he caught Penny's voice behind him.

His pulse surged like a teenager in heat. Last night had to be the end of it. She laughed deep and throaty, and he twitched. Grabbing his cup of coffee, he turned, ready to do battle, and found her walking with Maggie and Brady.

"How's Sam?" Brady searched Luke's eyes.

"We're waiting for the doctor to come in and let us know the test results." Luke glanced at Penny. She stood there as if nothing had happened between them.

Nothing had changed. That was how he had wanted it, after all.

"Amber's with him?" Maggie shook her head and smiled. "That girl... I'm amazed you were able to tear her away from his side last night. Penny said it was a good thing you were there for Sam."

"I'm glad I was there, too." Luke felt the collar on his black T-shirt tighten around his throat. "Sam never told me he was having heart problems or I would have been more diligent." And not been having sex in the closet.

"You know Sam," Penny said. "The strong, silent types rarely give you a clue into their hearts."

He narrowed his eyes on her. This wasn't the first time she'd referenced Sam as if she knew him better than just another person in the small town where they grew up. Everyone he kept in touch with had alluded to the fact that Penny got around. Hopping from one bed to another. Was Sam's one of those beds?

It wasn't inconceivable. The number of eligible men in Tawnee Valley, and even in Owen, dropped off after high school. Although the farmhouse looked as if a monk lived there, Sam might have had a booty call or two.

"Which room is he in?" Brady drew Luke's attention away from Penny, who had started to give him a strange look.

"I was just heading back there." Luke turned and walked with Brady down the hallway. Penny and Maggie chatted lightly behind them.

"You could have called me last night," Brady said.

"Ha! And interrupted your wedding night? No way." Luke took in a breath. "There wasn't much you could have done. Sam wasn't in immediate danger. They just wanted to monitor him overnight and run tests in the morning. Besides, they won't tell us anything unless Sam lets them."

"I'm glad you were here to take care of things." Brady stopped him. "What do you know about his heart?"

"He said you knew about the X-ray." At Brady's nod, Luke continued, "Glad to be in the loop. His problems could be caused by a number of possibilities. Until the test results are back, they won't be able to determine a course of treatment."

"How bad could it be?" Brady glanced back at Maggie and Penny, who had stopped discreetly a little farther down the hall.

The fainting had him most alarmed. Heart failure. Structural issues. But it could be just dehydration.

Luke took in a deep breath and released it. "Honestly, it could be as simple as monitoring and as complicated as a heart transplant."

"Damn."

"We won't know anything until the doctor comes in."

"Right." Brady ran a hand over his dark hair. "Right. Let's go, then."

When Luke glanced at her, Penny's insides turned molten. Luke had definitely improved with age and had gone about proving that to her with a fierce determination that had kept her up all night. If it weren't for his glances that seemed to be trying to dissect her, she would be afraid of falling for him again and begging him not to leave her. As if that would happen.

"Earth to Penny." Maggie waved a hand in front of Penny's eyes, breaking her view of Luke's butt in denim.

"Sorry. Did I miss something?" Penny blinked and tried to maintain an air of innocence.

"You aren't fooling me for one minute, Penny Montgomery." Maggie took her arm as the men started to move again. "I've known you practically all my life and I know when you've done the naughty."

"The naughty?" Penny laughed. "Good lord, woman, just call it what it is. Sex. S-e-x. Sex. Down-and-dirty, in-and-out sex. Which you should know because everyone is assuming you had sex last night, too."

"Shh. We're in a hospital, for goodness' sake." Maggie looked around as if a group of avenging nuns would descend on them.

"Yes, and it was good." Penny smirked. Damn good, if truth be told. She'd known that Luke had ruined her from falling in love ever again, but she'd hate it if he ruined her for sex, too.

"Hey." Maggie pulled her to a stop. Her hazel eyes searched Penny's. "He's not seeing anyone…."

Penny laughed. "You sound like Bitsy. You do know that I have a shop to run and he has a medical thingy hundreds of miles away, right? How's that supposed to work without the capability of time travel?"

"If you are in love, there are ways."

"Spoken like a true romantic." Penny tugged Maggie forward. "I'll just have to reserve myself for my weekly Winchester brothers viewing and let you stay the hopeless romantic."

"You know *Supernatural* won't be on the air forever." Maggie turned into the room.

"That's why I own the DVDs." She wiggled her eyebrows. "More Sam and Dean all to myself."

Penny couldn't make Maggie believe that she was determined to stay alone for the rest of her life. Okay, maybe not alone. She had Maggie and Amber, and she had Brady by marriage and any little ones that would come along. She'd be happy with that as long as they stayed right around the block.

Her heart pinched. Brady could have to move with his job. Even though he claimed he wanted to settle down in Tawnee Valley, how long would he be happy with small-town life? If Maggie left, where would Penny be?

God, she never got this emotional, even with lack of sleep. She'd deal with them moving if it happened. She turned the corner into the almost-full hospital room. Sam and Amber sat on the bed, and Luke and Brady stood beside Dr. Sanchez. Maggie joined Brady, who wrapped his arm around her.

There was no place for her. She glanced once at Luke, who had his head down over the chart the doctor had given him. She didn't belong with him. Taking a deep breath and ignoring the choking tears in the back of her throat, she left the room and the only family she had.

Dr. Sanchez was good at her job.

Luke didn't question that, even as he reviewed all her notes and the test results and cardiologist reports from St. Mercy in Springfield from last night and this morning. He wasn't looking for errors, just making sure that what she was saying was correct. Maggie had taken Amber to find some ice cream for Uncle Sam, while Brady and Luke stayed to listen to the doctor.

Luke checked the picture from the echocardiogram they had performed this morning. The still images had the measurements marked, showing the aortic valve. This wasn't what Luke had been expecting. His hand quaked as he turned to the next page. "Why didn't you mention the murmur last night?"

"Dr. Ward, you are well aware of HIPAA." Dr. Sanchez waited for his acknowledging nod before continuing. She couldn't release any information without Sam's consent, which he obviously hadn't given. "Everything points to severe aortic stenosis. We'd like to get Sam on the schedule in the next few days for surgery at St. Mercy Hospital in Springfield."

"Is this because of the enlargement of his heart?" Brady leaned against the windowsill with his arms crossed. His brow furrowed as he assessed the situation.

"Most likely the doctor who examined the X-ray couldn't tell that only the left side was enlarged from too much blood." Dr. Sanchez started writing on her chart. "That's why they strongly suggested that Sam go to a cardiologist, but I'm sure they told him not to worry. Some athletic men have slightly larger hearts, and for them it's nothing to worry about."

Sam had remained silent while the doctor spoke in her no-nonsense manner. Luke wanted to berate Sam for not following up, for not calling him to talk about his medical problems. Luke was training to be a cardiologist. The one person Luke had never understood— besides Penny—was Sam. Hell, maybe Sam and Penny were meant for each other. They both drove him nuts.

"I guess we'll cancel the trip." Brady looked at his phone. "I've already got the time off work, so I should be able to help out around the farm while Sam's recovering."

Before Luke could speak up, Sam said, "Who says I'm having the surgery?"

Dr. Sanchez held the chart to her chest and stared at Sam with dark, serious eyes. "If you were asymptomatic, we might be able to treat with drugs or even wait awhile, but your heart valve has already started to calcify. The fainting was only the beginning of your problems. If you don't have the surgery, you could go into heart failure."

Sam kept his lips together tightly. Not a single word. Just as he'd done all those times the principal had called him to the school for Luke's misconduct. Just as he had when he'd had to come to the police station to pick up Luke after a fight off campus. It was as if Sam just stopped caring at some point.

"I'm staying here." Luke stared into Sam's eyes, daring him to contradict him. Wanting him to. "I'll take family emergency leave to help out at the farm and help Sam out after his surgery."

"You need to get back to being a fancy doctor." Sam pushed up out of the chair.

"Brady deserves to go on his honeymoon and you need surgery."

"I'm fine. I don't even need to be here now."

"Bull." Luke saw red. "Of all the stupid, arrogant things you could do.... Do you think you are invincible? That you won't die if you don't have this surgery?"

Sam went lockjaw again. His face was stone.

"I'll let you discuss this in private." Dr. Sanchez backed out of the conversation. "I'll have the nurse call St. Mercy's to set up the necessary procedures."

The door shut behind her, leaving the cold silence. Luke didn't drop his gaze from Sam's eyes. If Sam could be stubborn, so could Luke. Sam was the tallest of the three, but he didn't have much height over Luke. They were practically eye to eye. Backing down wasn't an option. He wasn't a child who Sam could order around anymore.

Brady sighed and sank into the chair. "Are you guys going to stare at each other all day? Because I'd like to go have lunch with my wife and daughter."

"I'd be happy to leave now—" Luke brushed his hand over his hair "—but I'm not going to let another stubborn Ward die because he didn't listen to what the doctor was saying. I know the statistics. I know the symptoms. The doctor wasn't being completely honest."

Sam narrowed his eyes. The muscle in his jaw twitched.

"You will die if you don't have the surgery." Luke kept his expression flat and emotionless. "Within a year or two. Maybe sooner. This isn't something you can brush off…unless you have a death wish."

"What do you know about running a farm?" Sam said quietly. "The time and effort? The brute strength required? The long hours—"

"I'm a freaking doctor, Sam. I've spent twenty hours on shift before, followed by being on call. I know all about long hours and sacrifice." Cold seeped through him, taking the heat out of his words. Luke sat on the edge of the bed and rubbed his hand over his chin. He was not giving up, but he needed another tactic. "You need the surgery, Sam. I'm not ready to dig any more six-feet-deep holes."

Sam turned to Brady, who dropped his gaze to his hands. "Luke's right, Sam. I'm not ready to bury any more family. If it will save your life, I don't know why we are even having this discussion."

"They want to cut into my body and mess with my heart." Sam's face screwed up as if he'd eaten something bad. "While they are in there, they are going to take out part of my heart and replace it with a fake valve."

"And you'll feel better and live longer," Luke said. "I don't see what the problem is."

Sam shook his head and leaned against the end table. His gaze fell to the floor. "What if I don't make it?"

Luke took in a deep breath. He'd gone through this with patients before. The fear of the unknown. He hadn't expected Sam to be afraid. Not the Sam who had taken on Brady and him as a young man. Who'd stood at their mother's and father's gravesites without tears in his eyes.

In Luke's world growing up, Sam was brave and uncompromising. He was stern and unyielding. But he was never afraid.

"This surgery is less invasive than open-heart surgery." Luke stopped acting like a younger brother and became the doctor. "Every surgery has risks, but the benefits of this surgery far outweigh them. You'll be down for a few weeks and then able to do some light work. Before you know it, you'll be full Sam again. Except you'll feel better."

Sam grunted. "I have been feeling a little sick lately."

Luke wanted to exclaim disbelief but he held it back. Most likely Sam had felt like hell for weeks before this collapse. But pushing Sam would get him nowhere. Luke always got so frustrated with Sam that he forgot and blew up, even now as an adult.

Luke placed his hand on Sam's shoulder. "We'll get through this, Sam. Together."

Chapter Seven

"Hey, there you are."

Penny turned toward Maggie's voice. She'd found a magazine in the waiting room with a semi-interesting article on Chris Hemsworth and had decided to read instead of mope. She didn't need to mope. No one to love meant no one to leave you when you least expected it, when you really needed them, when you were starting to trust them again.

"I looked all over for you." Maggie sat down next to Penny and glanced at the article and the picture of Chris without his shirt on. "Nice." She smiled. "They are finishing up Sam's paperwork now, so we should be out of here soon. Then we're going to stop and grab some lunch before heading to the farm."

"What's the verdict?" Penny's stomach clenched. If Sam was okay, Luke would go back to his life in St. Louis.

If Sam wasn't, then Luke would hang around for a while. She wasn't sure which she wanted.

"Sam needs heart valve surgery." Maggie took in a deep breath. "Luke is insisting on staying and handling everything and that Brady and I go on our vacation after the surgery, while Sam is recovering. But I don't know. Sam and Brady were just starting to get to know each other again and if something happens to Sam…"

Penny took Maggie's hand. "We've gotten through worse before."

Maggie nodded and looked up at the ceiling as if to stop tears from forming. "But Sam's young and strong and we didn't even know he was sick."

"Sometimes it's like that." Penny could see her mother's drawn face twisted and ravaged from the years of abuse. For all she knew, her mother was dead. She shook off the image. "He's otherwise healthy. He'll get through this."

"Brady and Luke are talking the logistics." Maggie brushed her hair behind her ear. "I don't know what's going to happen, but would you be willing to help out while we are out of town? I can't imagine Luke being able to do everything by himself."

"He's perfectly capable." Penny shifted in her seat. "But I'll do what I can."

Maggie stared out the window into the blue sky. Some thought must have made her happy because she smiled softly. "It wouldn't be so bad."

"What's that?"

"Getting back together with Luke."

Penny laughed sharply as her heart ached. "I don't do relationships. I keep my options open. You never know when a hottie like Thor here will roll up into town. It'd be a shame to have to waste the eye candy because I'm *with* someone."

"You don't fool me for a minute, Penny." Maggie glanced down the hallway before returning her hazel gaze to Penny. "You talk a good game, but I know you. I know how much you loved Luke in high school. I don't know all of what happened between you two, but it couldn't have been too bad if he was willing to sleep with you last night."

"We didn't sleep." Penny winked, trying to throw off Maggie's speech. She was hitting a little too close to Penny's heart.

"You know what I mean." Maggie tightened her hold on Penny's hand. "I know you aren't happy with the way things are. You may enjoy other men, but I've never seen you light up the way you do when Luke is nearby. I know you've been hurt, but maybe it's time to heal a little. Maybe this is the second chance you need."

"Second chances like that are pretty rare." Penny looked out the window as a small brown bird flew by. If she let Luke in, he'd hurt her because she actually could love him. "And you got the only second chance we're going to see. Don't worry about me. I've got all the men I need in my life right now."

Maggie looked skeptical and opened her mouth.

"I swear, Maggie. I'm happy the way things are. I don't need anything more."

"Weren't you the one who said it wasn't about need?"

"That was to get you laid." Penny stood and brushed the wrinkles out of her slacks. "I'm doing just fine on that part."

Maggie stood. "This discussion isn't over."

"Yeah, it is. I don't need Luke and he doesn't need

me. We had a good time together. It's all good. Now, what's the plan? Is there food to be had?"

Maggie shook her head. "Come on."

When they got to the room, Penny's gaze met Luke's. He gave a hint of a smile, but the wrinkles on his forehead betrayed his worry. She hoped that Sam pulled through. Losing both his parents had devastated Luke. He couldn't lose Sam, too.

"I take it you guys have this all sorted?" Maggie asked as she touched Amber's dark hair.

Amber pouted. "We're going to Disney."

"You were excited for this trip, Squirt," Penny said.

"But who's going to take care of Uncle Sam after his surgery?" Amber turned to Penny. "You'll take care of him, won't you, Penny?"

Penny glanced around the room. Sam didn't make eye contact. Luke was intensely watching for her answer. Brady and Maggie just smiled indulgently.

"You always take real good care of me when I'm sick." Amber reached out and took both of Penny's hands. "If I know you'll be there, I might be able to have fun while I'm gone."

Amber's face was hopeful. Penny knew that no matter what she said Amber would have fun at Disney, but if it helped to get her on the plane without causing Maggie too much grief...

"You know I'll do whatever I can." Penny squeezed Amber's hands. "But you have to promise to have fun."

"Only if you call every night with an update."

"You drive a hard bargain." Penny bit out a laugh. Amber narrowed her eyes as if Penny weren't taking her seriously. "Sure. I'll check in with Luke every day and then call you."

"Check on Uncle Sam," Amber clarified.

Penny glanced over to Luke. "Your uncle Luke will be there—"

"I want you to."

"That's enough, young lady," Brady finally spoke up. "Penny has promised. Now let's go get something to eat and then get Sam set up at home. We have a lot to do to prepare for Sam's surgery and while we're on our trip."

Luke's eyes never left Penny's. Her pulse throbbed. She didn't know what he was searching for, but she didn't have anything left to hide. She wasn't Luke's girl anymore. He was just another notch on her lipstick case. Even though she'd have to talk to him and maybe even see him, nothing else was going to happen. A few weeks and he'd be gone and out of her life again.

Maybe she was the one with a heart condition. She rubbed the ache in her chest.

The surgery was set for Wednesday. Frankly it couldn't come soon enough. Keeping Sam indoors was proving to be a feat even for both Brady and Luke combined.

"You need to stay off your feet and rest." Brady shoved Sam toward the living room. "Play Xbox or watch a movie."

"I'm not an infant. I can do more than sit on my butt."

Brady headed back to the kitchen to talk to Maggie.

"Not if you want to live." Luke stood in the doorway. "We all grew up on this farm and each of us has done these chores a million times. I'm not sure why you think we're going to mess something up."

Sam grumbled something under his breath as he plopped in the worn-out recliner and grabbed the remote. Hopefully killing zombies on the Xbox would make Sam content to stay inside. He could pretend they were Brady and Luke if he really wanted to take out his anger. Lord knew that Luke had pretended they were Sam when he was younger. Luke turned and nearly ran over Penny.

"Sorry," he said. His breath caught in his throat as she looked up at him, startled.

"It was my fault," she muttered.

They'd barely spoken since the morning at the hospital. Apparently where Maggie and Amber went, Penny wasn't far behind. The three ladies worked on scrubbing the house, while he and Brady worked on straightening up the outside. Mom would have been thrilled that her house was being put back in order. They needed to get ahead on the farm chores for the days that Sam would be in the hospital for his surgery and recovery.

The unfortunate side effect was that Luke kept running into Penny, both figuratively and literally. Every touch caused his pulse to kick into overdrive. The house wasn't that big, which meant everyone was in everyone's way. It also meant that he hadn't been alone with Penny since the night of the wedding.

Penny still stood in front of him, looking at him with her brown eyes that always carried a hint of a devilish glint in them.

They weren't going to have sex again, he reminded himself for the tenth time that day. The night of the wedding was a one-time deal, but his body clearly had misread the memo.

"Did you need something?" Penny asked. A hint of a smile tugged at her lips.

Did he need something? How 'bout a convenient closet or bed for an hour or two? "No, I'm just heading out to work on the fence."

"Sounds exciting." She stretched her arms over her

head, which pushed her breasts against her tight black T-shirt.

His pants tightened and he had to restrain from adjusting himself.

"I get to clean the living room," she said in a fake excited voice. "Maybe afterward we can go beat laundry down on the rocks in the creek? Won't that be fun?"

Luke chuckled. "Better than gathering up the pigs for market."

"At least when Maggie and Brady leave, we can slack off once in a while." She leaned in conspiratorially. "I hid a package of ice cream bars in the back of the freezer behind a bag of frozen broccoli."

"Always thinking ahead—that's what I like about you, Montgomery." Luke relaxed.

"Someone has to." Penny took a deep breath and looked around. "Back to dusting. Yay?"

As she passed by him, he grabbed her hand. She looked at him with a question in her eyes.

"Thanks." Luke released her hand and flexed his still tingling fingers.

Penny winked. "Anytime."

Things with Penny were less complicated right now than his relationship with Sam. He really did appreciate that she got it. He knew, even though she didn't say it, that she did.

Penny's relationship with her grandma had always been similarly tense. They'd called her Grandma Tilly the Battle Ax.

She'd been old and alone when Penny's mother had dropped Penny off at her doorstep. Penny was more rambunctious than most kids and everyone knew that Tilly wasn't happy about having to raise her granddaughter. The stricter Tilly got, the wilder Penny got.

They were opposites in everything. Luke remembered the endless nights on a blanket staring up at the stars with Penny lying beside him. They'd talk about her grandma and Sam—the people who had gotten stuck with caring for Penny and Luke. They vowed that they'd never make anyone feel the way their caregivers made them feel. Like inconveniences instead of kids hurting from the loss of their parents.

He shook his head. Such thoughts didn't help anyone. He needed to focus on the farm and on getting Sam better. Not on Penny.

Chapter Eight

The days passed quickly, and before Luke knew it, it was Wednesday. Luke had driven Sam and Brady the hour to the hospital in Springfield. Everything ran smoothly. Checking Sam in. The staff preparing him for surgery. Watching them take him away.

Luke found himself once more in the hospital waiting room, this time with Brady. They talked for a little bit, but there wasn't much new to say because they'd spent the past few days working together.

Luke missed Penny's presence. She'd wished them the best last night before leaving and said she'd check in. He wished she were here now. She could always distract him, whether it was through flirting, having sex or just sitting and talking.

Now all he could do was run through the surgery in his mind's eye. Noting all the things that needed to happen. Everything that could go wrong. The steps to fix the mistakes. When he'd run through the procedures three times, he rubbed his face and turned to look to see what Brady was doing.

Brady had his laptop out and was working on some spreadsheet with numbers and formulas that Luke would need a business degree to understand. Luke pulled out his iPhone and scrolled through the emails he'd missed over the past few days. The signal out at the farm was questionable. Sometimes he received his emails, and other times, the battery drained from trying to connect to the server.

"Dr. Ward?"

Luke looked up at the nurse in scrubs. "Yes?"

"Sam is in recovery. The doctor would like to talk to you and your brother."

Luke glanced over to where Brady had been. His laptop was back in its case, but Brady wasn't there.

"Sorry, had to use the bathroom." Brady came down the hall toward them. "Everything okay?"

"Sam's out and in recovery." Luke took a deep breath. A lot of things still could go wrong, but the worst part was over.

After another hour, Luke had all the post-op information and had talked to Sam briefly. On the way home, he and Brady talked about the surgery and what they needed to do to prepare for Sam's homecoming in a few days.

When Luke pulled the car up to Maggie and Brady's house, Brady turned to him.

"Do you want to come in for a little bit? Maybe for some dinner? Maggie's a great cook."

Luke looked past Brady to the lights in the old Victorian's windows. He could see Maggie and Amber heading to the door to greet Brady. "Nah, you go ahead.

It's been a long day. You'll need to start packing for your trip."

"You sure?" Brady wasn't just being nice. He was sincere, but Luke wasn't in the mood for company.

"Yeah, we'll see each other tomorrow."

"'Night." Brady got out and without a backward glance walked into his family's arms.

Luke remembered what that felt like. To hug someone who cared more about what you were feeling than their own agenda.

It had been a long time since he'd felt that way. Dating in med school had been hard. He'd dated other med students mostly and everyone was mainly concerned about their grades and their shifts. No one really worried about anyone except themselves.

He didn't have what Brady had. Someone who would welcome him with open arms. His gaze went to the direction of Penny's house. It was only a block away.

Penny stared at the inventory screen of the online auction. It had a few good pieces that would look wonderful in What Goes Around Comes Around. A pair of gilded-and-silvered metal vases from nineteenth-century France and a seventeenth-century Italian writing desk had captured her attention. Although they were a bit ornate for her local customers, the tourists loved finding these types of treasures in her little shop.

Most of her inventory consisted of American furniture, artwork and tableware. But she loved to have a few older pieces from across the ocean for interest. People would come in to look at the vases and notice a set of silver or glassware that their grandma had and buy that instead.

She put in her bids and stretched. Flicker perked up

at her feet and looked at her hopefully with his giant brown eyes.

"No, I'm not taking you for a walk, you overgrown mop."

Flicker wagged his tail, knocking it against the table leg.

"If I'd known you were going to weigh almost as much as me, I would have let Brady take you back to the farm." When Brady had shown up with a surprise dog for Amber, Maggie had blown a gasket. Penny had stepped in and offered to keep the puppy. At the time, it had seemed easy and Amber loved the dog. Having never had a puppy before, Penny had been in for a treat.

The dog looked up at her with utter devotion. Penny couldn't resist an answering smile.

"Go back to sleep and maybe later we'll get a quick walk."

Flicker jumped up and headed to the door.

"Not now." Why did she say the word *walk?* "Flicker." The dog growled and then barked.

"What's—"

Someone knocked on the door. Most likely Amber or Maggie. They'd spent the afternoon together working on a new scrapbook for Amber. Penny shut her laptop.

When she opened the door, she didn't see anyone for a moment.

"Hey."

She jumped and looked to her right. Luke stood in the shadows. "You startled me."

"Sorry about that."

Flicker rushed out the door and sniffed at Luke. Luke rubbed the dog's head, and the poor thing turned to putty in his hand. Penny was way too intimately familiar with the feeling.

"This must be the legendary Flicker." Luke didn't look up at her as Flicker put his front paws on Luke's chest in an effort to lick his face. His jeans, slung low on his hips, drew her attention. He filled them out nicely. She forced her gaze up to his button-down white shirt.

She ran her suddenly damp palms over her pink cotton shorts. Expecting to be alone this evening, she'd already changed into her pajamas. She hadn't thought to grab her sweater before answering the door since it was probably Maggie or Amber, and her comfy pink cotton tank didn't help against the cool evening air.

"Did you want to come in?" Penny grabbed Flicker's collar and tugged him off Luke. "It's a bit chilly out here."

Luke's eyes caught on her breasts before lifting to meet her eyes. "Sure."

He followed her into the house.

"Have a seat. I'll put Flicker out in the backyard." She motioned to the living room and hauled the dog out through the kitchen door. When she got back, Luke was staring at the pictures on the wall.

Her heart stopped. Most of the pictures were of Maggie, Amber and her, but the one he was focused on was the one of Luke and her. The night hadn't mattered and hadn't been anything special. It could have been any night or every night, but that picture showed how much in love they had been.

"Can I get you something to drink?" She wanted to ask why he was here. What had happened with Sam? Did he feel this intense, almost-drunk feeling when she was near, as she did? It made her feel comfortable and on edge in the same moment. "I have a beer or I could make some tea."

"No." He reached out and stroked a finger down the picture.

She shuddered as if he'd touched her. Goose bumps rose on her arms. It wasn't the chill in the air affecting her. It was the electric current running between them that had her body humming like a live wire.

He turned toward her. His blue eyes glowed in the dim light the lamp offered. "Are you expecting someone?"

"No. I was just working some before going to bed." She didn't normally have anyone over during the week. Before last weekend, it had been quite a while since she'd hooked up with someone. She was busy with work and helping with Maggie's wedding. It definitely didn't have anything to do with the fact that Luke would be coming home.

He glanced over her shoulder, down the hallway. A thrill shot through her. He knew exactly where her bedroom was. They hadn't had the chance to use it very often as teenagers, but he'd snuck in a few times. He was the only guy who had made it to her bedroom.

Suddenly she felt vulnerable and naked.

It had nothing to do with her state of dress. She wouldn't care if she were literally naked in front of Luke, but he'd been inside her head and heart as a teenager. Maggie knew her, but not as Luke did…or, rather, had.

"Sorry I interrupted you." Luke sank into the worn recliner.

"I had just finished up when you knocked." She hesitated in the doorway for a moment before she shook herself. She wasn't shy when it came to men, but something about Luke threw her off her game. She walked into the room and sat across from Luke with her legs tucked up under her. "What's up?"

"Sam's surgery went well." He combed his hand through his hair.

"It must have been a long day for you." Her heart beat mercilessly against her rib cage. Why was he here? To talk? To vent? To have sex?

"I just dropped off Brady."

To not be alone? She'd been there many times.

His fingers stroked sensually down the ruby-red glass of the Egermann Bohemian perfume bottle on the end table next to him. It didn't take much for her to remember those fingers tracing the vein in her neck.

"And since you were in the neighborhood, you thought you'd pass along the news of Sam?" Not bloody likely. This whole week had been an exercise in chastity. Something she wasn't entirely comfortable or familiar with. They'd never had a moment alone, which was probably good. If they had, she would have dragged him somewhere and to hell with her promises to her heart to keep him at arm's length for the duration of his stay. Besides, all promises were meant to be broken.

"Something like that." He seemed way too fascinated with the glass. It was as if he was trying to put her on edge. Draw her attention to the fingers that had provided her with hours of pleasure.

Keeping up this conversation was pointless. If he were here to drive her mad with desire, it was working. And since he hadn't touched her, she'd be on her own tonight. He'd hardly acknowledged the fact that she was barely dressed. If they weren't going to get busy, she would have to work through her desires by herself. She started to stand up.

"Wait." He held up his hand, still looking at the bottle.

She returned to her seat, not because he'd ordered her to, but because she was curious.

"Tell me about this." His words were so quiet and his voice so deep she almost didn't hear him.

"It's a ruby perfume bottle made by Egermann after 1860 in Bohemia."

Luke lifted his gaze to hers. "Penny?"

"Yes?"

"Give me its story."

She drew in a deep breath. When she was younger, she'd been fascinated with the antiques in her grandma's store. She'd spent countless hours there, wondering where everything came from, making up their stories to make them so much more than they were: things left behind by people who were either gone or no longer wanted them. "The real one?"

"Give me your story."

She hadn't thought up stories in years. Something in his lost look made her want to draw him into her embrace and just hold him for hours until whatever haunted him went away. He hadn't asked for that, but she could give him a story. "The year was 1867. There was a man who desired a woman very much."

He watched her with an intensity that took her breath away. "Go on."

She licked her lips and continued, "She was everything to him, but she didn't see him. Not as a man. Not as a person. One day he saw her standing in a store. In her hands she held that very perfume bottle. She stroked it with longing and smelled deeply of the perfume, which had the rich scent of jasmine in it. He could tell she wanted it very much."

Luke stood and crossed the room. He hunkered down

in front of her. His knuckles brushed her bare leg. "Tell me more."

She swallowed. "The woman put it back because she didn't have enough money for it. After she left the store, he went to the bottle and spent every last coin he had in his pocket on it, confident that with it, he would finally have her love. That night he went to her house and presented her with the bottle."

"What did she do?" He brushed her hair behind her ear and cradled her head in his hand.

Her breath whispered past her lips. "She invited him inside."

"Will you?" He pulled her head down toward his. She didn't resist.

"Will I what?"

He stopped before their lips touched. "Let me in."

Penny closed the distance between their mouths, answering him the only way she knew how. Their lips met and clung together. Sparks flew behind her eyes. Her skin tingled with the longing to be touched. Liquid heat flowed through her and pooled in the center of her.

Without breaking the kiss, he rose and took her into his arms. This was crazy. Foolish. The future was an unknown. The past was gone. This was perhaps the worst mistake she could make. But right now, Luke was the only thing that mattered to her. This connection. His mouth, his body, his essence…the fuel for this raging passion within her.

Chapter Nine

Luke hadn't known what to expect when he knocked on Penny's door. He wouldn't fool himself into believing his intentions had been any less than kissing Penny until he managed to release the devil that had been riding him since their night together.

He pulled away from the kiss. Her body was flush against his, her chest rising and falling with every breath. He ran a finger under the strap of her tank top.

"I never figured you for a pink-cotton girl." He rested his forehead against hers.

"My black and red lace teddies are all in the wash." Her fingers tangled in his hair.

"Liar." He pulled her from her chair and sat back on the floor with her on his lap.

"You've discovered my secret." She ran her fingers along the neckline of his shirt until she reached the top button. With a flick of her finger, she released it. "I have an all-encompassing passion for cotton pajamas. Shorts, pants, T-shirts, tank tops. I can't get enough of them."

He ran his hands up her bare legs until he brushed the cotton of her shorts.

"I can't let you leave here," she said. Her expression was serious, but the glint in her eyes ruined the effect.

He cupped her bottom and pulled her tight against his hardness. "Why is that?"

"Because you know at least one of my secrets." She dipped her head to kiss his neck. A pulse of pure heat went straight through his body. She pushed him back until he lay flat on the carpet. "I have to find out what else you know."

Her fingers wove with his and pressed his hands into the floor. He could easily overpower her if he wanted to. She took his mouth with hers. Her tongue danced with his. His blood ran hot through his veins and his brain began to short-circuit. His fingers twitched with the desire to explore her lush body. She released his mouth and stared down into his eyes.

"What if I'm not willing to talk?" Luke leaned up and nipped her chin.

She smiled wickedly. "We'll see about that."

Penny took her time removing his clothes, button by button, kissing every inch of skin she uncovered until Luke couldn't think straight. By the time she had him fully naked, he was sensitive everywhere. The slightest breeze from the open window made him stiffen with desire. He allowed her to do what she wanted, enjoying her attentions more than he probably should.

When he couldn't take any more, he lifted her top over her head and helped her out of her shorts and underwear. Having her naked skin against his was the most enticing feeling in the world. She was intoxicating. So sure and aware of herself as a sexual creature.

He wanted too much from her. He knew that. He wanted everything, every piece of her down to her very soul. But it was impossible. He'd learned that lesson years ago as a boy. As a man, he would take what she offered and enjoy her without reading too much into her moans of delight and her desire to please him.

After covering him with a condom, she hovered above him. Aphrodite herself. Her flesh pressed intimately with his. He had so many things he wanted to say, needed to tell her. Things she should know. She was one of a kind. In nine years, he hadn't been able to replace her in his mind or in his heart. No one compared to her.

"So beautiful." He reached up and stroked the side of her face.

Her passion-glazed eyes met his. She took his hand, pressed her lips against his fingertips. "I want to come apart with you."

She came down on him. They both gasped in air as if they were starving for it. She set a slow rhythm, but he couldn't take it. He grabbed her hips and set a new pace. He watched her every expression until she tightened all around him, taking him over the edge with her.

She collapsed on his chest. Both of them worked to catch their breaths.

A laugh escaped Penny.

"Not something a guy likes to hear after sex," he grumbled and kissed the top of her hair.

She rested her chin on her hands on his chest to look at him. Her brown eyes sparkled. "Trust me when I say that laugh *wasn't* about your performance. And may I say, 'bravo'?"

"You can applaud if you like." He smiled and pushed her hair from her face. "But I think you did most of the work."

"I wouldn't call it work." She squirmed against him and raised an eyebrow. "But you know, if you have some pent-up energy you need to expend—"

She squealed as he flipped her onto her back.

He leaned over her, his hand tracing along the side of her breast. "Since you seem in the mood to laugh, let's see if I can remember where your tickle spots are."

Penny hummed as she dusted the shelves of her shop the next morning. She still wasn't entirely sure why Luke had come over last night, but she definitely wasn't complaining after the christening of her living room rug.

"Penny dear, did you get bit by a mosquito?" Bitsy Clemons was making her morning rounds. With only a few shops on Main Street, Bitsy could spend a lot of time in each and still make it home for lunch.

Penny reached up and touched her neck. "Uh, yeah, nasty little buggers."

"We need to spray for them before they get bad this summer." Bitsy wandered down the aisle to the jewelry trays.

Penny glanced in one of the antique mirrors on the wall. Sure enough, she had a huge hickey from Luke as a greeting card this morning. Damn.

Luke had left sometime during the night and she'd crawled into bed exhausted. This morning, she'd overslept and managed to roll into the shower and pull on some clothes just in time to get to the shop for opening. She'd forgotten to look for collateral damage.

The bell above the door rang—hopefully announcing Bitsy's departure.

Some damage Penny had noticed—thankfully. The rug burns on her knees were discreetly hidden by her slacks. Bitsy would have a heart attack if she'd seen exactly how Penny had gotten those puppies. She chuckled.

"Someone's in a happy mood," Luke's voice slipped over her like a satin nightie, causing her knees to turn to gelatin.

She grabbed a shelf to hold herself steady before turning to face him. "Well, I did get lucky last night."

He moved in, drawing her closer with the crisp scent of his cologne. "Maybe you are on a winning streak."

"God, I hope so." She smiled up at him.

He leaned toward her as if to kiss her. The tinkling of jewelry being sorted alerted him that they weren't alone. He stiffened and took a step back. "Maggie, Brady and Amber went next door to grab something for their trip. They should be here in a minute. I'm driving them to the airport and they insisted on saying goodbye. Afterward I'm heading to the hospital to sit with Sam for a while."

"Cool." What power did Luke have that he always made her feel awkward when he was near? She didn't know what to do with her hands or how to stand. Which was ridiculous because this was Luke. He'd seen and touched every inch of her body.

"Is that Luke Ward?" Bitsy came hurrying down the aisle as if Luke might take off at the sight of her. Her blue floral skirt billowed out behind her like a cape.

Luke gave Penny a help-me look.

Penny just smiled and returned to dusting.

"My goodness, you've grown into quite the man. I remember when you were knee high to a grasshopper."

Bitsy eyed Luke as if he was the prize pig at the county fair. If he weren't careful, she might start poking and testing his muscles. Penny covered a laugh with a cough. "And a doctor, too."

"It's a pleasure to see you again, Mrs. Clemons."

"Oh, stop." Bitsy blushed to the roots of her silver hair and waved her hand. "We're all adults here. You can call me Bitsy."

Luke smiled. "What are you looking for today, Bitsy?"

"I just come to browse and help Penny in her quest for true love." Bitsy placed her hand on Luke's arm. "I know you two were involved once upon a time, but really she needs to settle down with someone before she's too old to have children."

Penny stopped her dusting. "True love? Kids? And here I thought you were just setting me up with men for the fun of it."

"What's wrong with kids?" Luke had a mischievous look in his eyes, as if he was enjoying her torture.

"Nothing's *wrong* with kids as long as they are someone else's." Penny raised her eyebrow, daring him to contradict her.

"Now, now, Penny. Take it from an old lady who never had kids of her own. One day you'll want kids and it will be too late." Bitsy nodded her head sagely. She'd married late in life and never had any children. She'd been friends with Penny's grandma and had always slipped Penny sweets when she came by to talk with Grandma Tilly.

"Don't worry, Bitsy. I have a few good years left if I want to push out a brat or two."

"Ticktock," Bitsy scolded. She glanced to the clock on the wall. "Oh, time to go see Mr. Martin. It was good seeing you, Luke, and if you have any single doctor friends, make sure to send them Penny's way."

They watched her scurry out of the store. Alone once again with Luke, Penny's heart fluttered. Talking about kids and men in front of Luke had been extremely awkward. But now that they were alone, they didn't have to talk at all.

He closed in on her, forcing her to look up to meet his eyes or stare at his chest. Hmm, decisions, decisions. It was such a fine chest. She sighed and met his eyes.

"Ticktock." He grinned down at her.

"Not you, too." She took a deep breath and her breasts grazed his chest. "I've got years before I even need to worry about that damned clock."

His fingers stroked a strand of hair that had escaped her messy bun. "Do you want children?"

"You offering?" She intended to throw him off. With him standing so near, her insides were pooling into liquid warmth that flowed through her whole body.

"Stop trying to distract me, Penny." He dipped his head slightly and she swore he was going to kiss her. Talk about distracting. "What are your future plans? What happens after right now?"

"I get lucky?" She flashed him a grin. She certainly hoped she would.

"What do you want?" he whispered close to her ear, stealing any breath she had left. His voice was rich and soothing. She swore she could listen to him read a dictionary and be turned on.

He pulled back. His blue eyes were dark pools, begging her to strip naked and dive in. He was close enough that his heat made her want to sway forward and rub against his warmth. She wanted him. 24/7.

"Do you want kids?" he asked.

Kids? A baby? With Luke's blue eyes and her red hair? Someone she could love and who would love her in return. Who would rely on her for everything. Who she would disappoint.

A shard of cold went through her.

"I—" She swallowed and stepped back against the shelf. Straightening, she slid away from him down the aisle. She didn't want these thoughts. She knew what she could and couldn't have, and a child was a *couldn't*. "I need to get back to work."

"I want children," Luke said as if she hadn't walked away from the conversation. "I want a wife and home and children. Someday."

Her chest ached. She didn't look back at him. Thinking of Luke with his future wife and their perfect house and perfect children was enough to make her want to lose her breakfast.

"That's great," Penny choked out and blinked back the burning tears in her eyes. "You'll make a great dad."

His hands rested on her shoulders. His touch brought on another surge of tears. "Penny—"

The bell on the door jingled and Brady's, Maggie's and Amber's voices broke their solitude. She heard his sigh before his hands slipped away. She rushed to the back into the storeroom and shut the door behind her. She took a great shuddering breath in and scolded herself.

Luke wasn't hers. In no universe would he be hers. She'd made sure of that years ago. So why did the thought of him with someone else burn through her stomach like a branding iron? She set down the duster and grabbed a tissue. After a few deep breaths, she pulled herself together.

Just because they were having some fun didn't give

her any hold over Luke. Just because she'd loved him once didn't mean she was in danger of being in love with him again. Just because the thought of a child, his child, made her clench up inside with longing didn't mean she wanted one.

She picked up the present she'd wrapped for Amber and opened the storeroom door, prepared to do battle.

Chapter Ten

Luke stepped out from behind the shelving and into the open part of the store, where the front desk and cash register were.

"Where's Penny?" Amber asked.

"She went into the back for something." Most likely to get away from him. She was upset and she had every reason to be. He didn't know why he'd pushed so hard. Maybe it was because Bitsy hadn't thought he'd be the right guy for Penny. If he had any single friends… Not in this lifetime. "I'm sure she'll be right out."

"Everything okay?" Maggie asked.

"Yeah." No, it wasn't. "Did you guys get what you needed?"

"We're all set," Brady said as he picked up a little blue bottle, which looked as if it might have once had medicine in it, off a shelf.

"I hear someone is going to Disney World." Penny

appeared. It was as if nothing strange had passed between them. She smiled at Amber and held out a little box, gift-wrapped and tied with a bow.

"For me?" Amber took the box and opened it very carefully.

Penny glanced up at him before returning her gaze to Amber. He saw how much she loved being around Amber. Why wouldn't she want that for herself? His heart beat a little harder with the thought of Penny with a baby in her arms. Would they already have a few kids if she'd come with him to university? He could imagine lying in bed with her on a Sunday morning with kids climbing onto the bed with them. One happy family.

He startled. He could have been happy with her, but not if he couldn't even be sure if the kids were his. What was so fundamentally broken with her that she couldn't be with just him? Hadn't he been enough? Lord knew he couldn't get enough of her. Even now.

"O.M.G. It's a Mickey necklace. Mom, it's a Mickey necklace." Amber brought him back to the here and now.

"I see that," Maggie said.

"Oh, thank you, thank you, thank you. I've always wanted one." Amber threw her arms around Penny and Penny squeezed her tight.

As soon as Amber released her to go show Brady, Penny looked at Luke. It was there in her eyes, that longing for something she couldn't have. Whether she told him she wanted children or not, that look told him everything. She wanted a child, but she was content holding her best friend's daughter as her own.

He kept his gaze on Penny as they all said their goodbyes. Brady's family would be gone for ten days and then they'd be back to help out again. After that, Luke could leave at that time if he wanted to. As they exited the shop, Penny met his gaze. He knew the only thing he wanted right now was her. And although she seemed to want him now, who's to say that tomorrow, she wouldn't want someone else?

"'Bout time you showed up." Sam lay in his hospital bed in a robe and hospital gown, looking distinctly uncomfortable. "When do I get out of this place?"

"You only had surgery two days ago," Luke sat in the chair next to the bed. "They want you to stay one more night."

"How am I supposed to get better with all these tubes in me?" Sam held up his IV with disdain. "This sucks."

"I'm sure it does." Luke looked out the window. Springfield wasn't nearly as big as St. Louis, but it was a decent size for the middle-of-nowhere Illinois. The surrounding buildings seemed dreary and worn-out.

"How's the farm?" Sam picked up the remote and flipped the channel on the TV. A news channel played in the background with the sound on mute.

"The animals are tended. The Baxter boys have been by to help with the fields."

John Baxter was a neighboring farmer who helped Sam out in the spring and fall during seeding and harvesting. His two sons went to the local community college and helped out year-round. Sam returned the favor by giving them bales of hay at baling time.

"That's good." Sam rubbed at the stubble on his chin. After a few minutes, he said, "I made an appointment with the cardiologist. His office is around the corner from the hospital."

"There isn't anyone closer?" An hour's drive both ways every day to the hospital to check up on Sam was annoying, especially because Luke kept going to Penny's before going home. Last night they'd barely spoken when he'd shown up at her door. He hadn't said a word, just took her in his arms. She'd pulled him into her dining room, where they'd made good use of the table and chairs. He had yet to see the inside of her bedroom. He barely managed any sleep before waking for the morning chores. "What about Dr. Patterson?"

"He retired. Tawnee Valley hasn't had a doctor in years, and Owen only has a handful of specialists. No cardiologists." Sam fluffed a pillow and shoved it behind his head.

Luke leaned forward, thinking of the ramifications of sick people having to go an hour just to get to their doctor. Most people would either just not go to the doctor at all or go to the emergency room rather than make the trip. Filling up the emergency room with people best seen in an office made it hard for the true emergencies to get in. The hospital in Owen must be a nightmare of never-ending patients.

"You get the tractor running?" Sam asked, interrupting Luke's thoughts.

"What? Yeah, it only needed a new fuse."

Sam nodded and continued to watch the TV.

Luke returned to his thoughts. It was bad enough that a lot of patients came from miles away to see specialists in the hospital he worked at in St. Louis, but those patients usually had a doctor close by who they could follow up with.

The population of Tawnee Valley and even Owen was skewed to an older than average age. Those people shouldn't have to sit in a car for an hour just to get some medical advice. Especially just for checkups to make sure nothing has changed or whether a new medicine was working or not.

"Anything new?" Sam said.

"What?" Luke turned to look at Sam.

Sam rarely spoke outside of direct questions and answers. He looked highly uncomfortable. "I'm stuck in a hospital bed watching bad TV. I'm bored."

Luke smiled. "You want me to bring you my laptop next time? It has solitaire on it."

"I better be going home tomorrow. If you won't take me, I'll hitch a ride." Sam shoved the remote away. "Or maybe Penny would come get me."

If Luke were a rooster, his feathers would be rustled. "Why would Penny do that?"

"She and I are a lot alike. Both alone." Sam closed his eyes and put his arm behind his head.

The idea of Sam and Penny together burned Luke deeper than thinking of her with any other man. Sam was his brother, his guardian. He was supposed to watch out for Luke, not steal his girl. Even if his girl had been a willing participant. "You won't have to call Penny because I'll be here."

"Good."

Luke sat for an hour more with Sam, answering his random questions and silently fuming. He couldn't get the image of Sam kissing Penny out of his head. The night of his graduation, he'd been outside with his friends when he went back into the house to get a drink. Through the kitchen door, he could see Penny with her hands around Sam's neck, her body tight against his. Her lips pressed against Sam's. Sam's hands had been on her hips.

He hadn't needed to see more. All that locker room talk. All the times Penny had talked him down from kicking some guy's ass for saying he was nailing her. It had all been true. What he had thought was love had been a lie.

All those hours they'd spent, dreaming and planning, had been for nothing. He was just another one of her guys. He just hadn't realized it.

The drive home didn't help his dark mood. If Sam and Penny did end up together, she'd be his sister-in-law. He'd have to see her with him at every family get-together. Participate in her and Sam's wedding as if he were happy to be there.

By the time he drove into Tawnee Valley, it was late. He could have gone straight to the farm and just skipped seeing Penny tonight, but that wasn't going to happen.

He parked his car in front of her house and stared at the dark street ahead of him. It was all in the past. He'd moved on. She'd moved on. What they were doing now…that was just for fun. Something to keep the boredom away.

It had taken him a year to get over the betrayal. But he'd never truly let it go. Maybe that was because he'd been so sure that they had been in love. He slammed his hand against the steering wheel. This was stupid.

The past shouldn't matter. Penny wasn't the same girl. She had solid roots in the community. A sensitive side that she rarely showed. So she enjoyed sex. Since when had that been a crime?

If she and Sam were involved, they didn't act like it. Even if they were just having sex, it would be a while before Sam was up to anything. This was ridiculous. Luke was here for only another week or so. He didn't have any hold over Penny or control over who she spent her time with.

But he'd make damned sure who she would spend her time with tonight.

Penny was just about to give up on Luke coming over when she heard a knock on the door. The fluttering in her stomach made her want to not answer. He was getting to her, and that could be very bad.

Sex didn't equal love in her world. But Luke…Luke was an intensity she couldn't deny.

She crossed the room to the door and pulled it open. Their eyes met. No matter if it was the first time or the thousandth time, when Luke came near her she melted.

She moved out of the doorway to let him in, as if she had a choice. In her heart she knew that anytime Luke wanted her, she would let him in. Into her home. Into her body. Into her heart.

He moved past her into the living room.

"Who are you sleeping with?" Luke asked as he sat on her couch. His long legs spread out before him.

His question took her aback, but she wasn't intimidated by it. It didn't prevent the pain that gouged her heart at his question. She remembered how easy it was for him to believe the worst in her. Did he worry that she was sleeping with someone else now? Was he afraid she couldn't juggle the workload? She curled up in the corner of the couch next to, but not touching, him. She let him stew a few minutes before meeting his gaze.

"Honey, I'm not sleeping with anyone." It was the God's honest truth. They hadn't slept together. They had mind-blowing sex and then he left to go out to the farm so he could rise with the roosters.

"You know what I mean."

"Someone's a little testy this evening." She stretched back and put her legs across his lap.

He met her eyes and held them. Every bit as serious as he sounded. "Are you having sex?"

"With you? Not yet." She gave him a wink. What was he after? If she played this game long enough, he'd get to his point sooner or later or give up entirely and get to the good part of the evening.

"I'm serious."

"I know you are." Penny sighed and put her arms behind her head. "What do you want from me, Luke? An oath of fidelity? My declaration of love?"

His eyes narrowed, but then he took in a deep breath and pulled her by her legs toward him. She went willingly. When he had her straddling his lap, he took both her hands and placed them on his shoulders. "This isn't normal for me."

"This position or this situation?" She cocked a grin at him. Her core pulsed.

"I'm supposed to be working right now."

"I know and I wish you'd get on with it already." She ran her hands down his T-shirt, feeling the hard muscles twitch beneath it.

"Penny, stop."

"Killjoy."

"I want to have a conversation with you."

"Why?" Penny traced the bottom edge of his shirt with her fingernail. "Why do we have to talk at all? What is there to say that would make any difference?"

"How about 'I care about you'?"

She held her breath, waiting for the *but*.

"I want to know that you take care of yourself. It seems like we skipped some of the important conversations to have before having sex." Luke placed his hands on her hips lightly.

"What kind of conversations?" she asked suspiciously.

"How many people have you been with?"

Her heart hitched. This seemed like a huge trap. "I don't want to play this game."

She moved to get off him, but his hands held her tightly.

"Okay, no numbers," he said. He clearly wasn't happy about it, though.

She stopped trying to move off him. The real number probably wasn't as high as he imagined it was. She had no reason to be ashamed of the amount of men she'd been with, but this was Luke. Her first and her latest.

"Have you always been safe?" His eyes delved into hers.

"Is this the doctor asking?" she teased, trying to ease the tension growing inside her.

"No, it's the man who's having sex with you and plans on doing it again. I know we are using condoms, but have you always?"

"Yes, always." She met his gaze head-on. If he wanted to know the details, why the hell not? "You?"

He nodded and his fingers relaxed their grip of her hips. "Do you get tested?"

She nodded and raised her eyebrow at him as if to say, *Do you?*

"Of course." He shifted slightly beneath her. "When was the last time you had sex?"

"You should know. You were there. Was I that forgettable?" She fake pouted and then winked, not able to resist trying to lighten this conversation. Why was he suddenly being so serious?

He pulled her in tightly against him. He was solid everywhere and it made her want him more. "With someone else."

She threaded her fingers through his hair. "Well, Doctor, let's see…. It was before the wedding, before planning the wedding, before Maggie and Brady got back together…. Was it spring last year or winter? Damn, it's been a while. Good thing you're here."

Leaning into him, she placed a kiss on his lips. His arms wrapped around her, holding her, and he opened his mouth beneath hers. Pleasure raced down her spine as his tongue brushed against hers. It was as if he were rewarding her for her answer. If those were the types of rewards he was doling out, he could ask away. He pulled back and she whimpered. His satisfied smile made her want to key him up and then leave him hanging as he was doing to her. The most sensual torture.

"I'm not done asking questions," he said.

"What if I'm done answering questions?"

"Fine. Ask me a question, then."

She sat back and thought for a moment. "When was your last serious relationship?"

For a moment, hurt flashed in his eyes. Was he remembering them? His smile didn't reach his eyes. "I haven't had time for serious."

That one hurt. This great guy hadn't had anyone in his life. What was the point of breaking it off if he didn't find that special someone who would be the woman he needed? She asked, "Semi-serious?"

He shook his head. This crazy feeling started in her chest, like a boa constrictor releasing its prey. She shouldn't feel this way about Luke. It was dangerous to even consider anything past tonight. She'd just end up more ruined.

"You?" he asked.

"Not even kind of serious." She met his eyes and could see the relief in them, but there was still some reserve. Something he was holding back.

"Have you loved anyone?" he asked.

Since you? She couldn't make her voice work, so she shook her head.

"Me neither." He relaxed against the couch and pulled her hips forward. "Do you think we are broken?"

"How do you mean?"

"Like the reason we can't love someone is because of the stuff we went through as kids?" Luke leaned his head back and looked up at the ceiling. "I was a mess after Mom and Dad died."

"You weren't that bad," she said softly and cradled his face in her hand.

"I was a walking disaster. I almost had to repeat a year in high school because my grades were so low. I picked fights with anyone who looked at me the wrong way—"

"You were hurt. You were lashing out."

He'd been a wounded animal. She'd recognized him as a kindred spirit right away.

"You were, too." He brushed her hair off her cheek and cradled the back of her head. "We should have self-destructed. Instead we came together."

"You needed someone. I needed someone." She shrugged. "We made sense."

"What about now?" He pulled her in close but held back from kissing her. His breath was warm against her lips. Tantalizing, teasing. "Do we make sense now, Penny?"

Heaven help her. Her eyes fluttered closed, waiting for him to take her. "Didn't we self-destruct back then?"

"I want you." He brushed his lips across hers. "I can't get you out of my head. When I'm sitting alone, I wish you were there to talk to. When I'm working on the farm, I want you there beside me."

"So you can push me in the mud?" She tried to inch forward, but he held her back.

"Can't you be serious for one minute?" He tsked and leaned down to nip at her neck.

She released a low moan as he hit a spot that made her whole body quake with desire. "I want you, Luke. Any way you want me. Anytime. I want you now. I'll want you tomorrow and the next day. I crave your touch and covet your time."

He pulled back and rested his forehead against hers. Their eyes locked. "What's happening?"

"Do we have to pick it apart?" she whispered. The ache in her core was driving her insane. "Do we have to analyze this? Can't it just be what it is?"

"But what is it?" Luke brushed his thumb over her bottom lip. "Is this just a sex thing? Or is more going on?"

Her hands started to shake, and deep in her chest that boa wrapped tightly around her heart again. She wanted to scream that she was unlovable. That even if he thought he was in love with her, it wouldn't last.

"Are you willing to admit that we have more than sex between us?" Luke brushed his lips against hers again.

"Do you want me to admit that I need you? Because that's not going to happen. I don't need anyone. I have my house, my business, my dog—"

"I'm not asking you to need me, Penny." Luke lifted her to her feet and stood before her.

"Then what do you want?"

"A chance. A date. To get to know the woman you

are and not the girl I knew." He stroked his knuckles down the side of her face. "I don't know where any of this is going. Or what's going to happen in a week. But I know I want to spend time with you."

"So you want to hang out without having sex?" She looked up at him through her eyelashes.

"Yes."

She smiled and raised her eyebrow. "No sex?"

"I'm sorry, but sex is definitely on the table…or the floor, if you prefer." Luke grabbed her hips and pulled her close. "Or even a bed. You do own one, right?"

"Of course I have a bed."

He wiggled his eyebrows wickedly. "Point the way."

She put her hand to his chest to stop him. "My bedroom is off-limits."

Wrinkles formed on his forehead. "You do live alone, right?"

"Yes, I live alone. My rules." She didn't want to tell him that it was her personal space and that to invite someone in was too scary.

"I'll go out with you and have sex with you, but not in my bedroom."

Luke held her hand against his heart. "Someday you'll have to let someone in."

She smiled sadly. Not today. Never again.

"Can I offer you a drink?" She took his hand in hers and led him through the dining room. With her other hand, she started unbuttoning her blouse. "There's a lovely view out of the kitchen."

"I don't think the view could get much lovelier."

"Keep up lines like that and I might let you take me to dinner."

"I can keep it up all night if you like."

Chapter Eleven

"I can walk myself." Sam shoved Luke away for the third time.

Luke ran his hand through his hair. "I'm not trying to hold your hand, you ninny. The gravel drive isn't a stable surface and you have steps up the porch."

"That I've been climbing since I was one." Sam gave him a menacing look when Luke stepped closer. "I'll be fine, but *you* won't if you keep trying to touch me."

"Fine." Luke held his hands up. "Just don't take one step past the downstairs bedroom."

Sam made a rude gesture and continued to plod his way to the house.

The screen door opened and Penny came out. Her ginger hair shone in the sunlight. She wore a pink tank top and a pair of cutoff jeans with sandals. Even though the days were warming up, the nights were still cool.

"I just finished putting away the groceries," she said as Sam shuffled past without even a look.

Clearly, Luke had misread the few times either of them had brought up the other. Seeing that kiss had colored his view. They barely acknowledged each other even when they were in the same room.

"Thanks, Penny." Luke leaned over and kissed her before going into the house. His chest felt warm; being able to claim her in public put him in a great mood. Before he'd left to pick up Sam, they'd had breakfast at The Rooster Café in Tawnee Valley. She'd even held his hand across the table. It was ridiculous how good that made him feel when hours before he'd been in heaven in her arms.

"I'll get dinner ready, but then I need to go into town." Penny shut the screen door and moved to the stove.

"You aren't going to eat with us?" Luke set down Sam's hospital bag and came up behind Penny. He pulled her back against him while she lit the stove under a pot with water and potatoes in it.

"I have to get some work done and put Flicker out."

He bit down lightly on the place where her shoulder and neck met. "What about later?"

"Sam's here. You are going to have your hands full. I've got a big day tomorrow at the store." She turned in his arms to face him. Her smile didn't quite reach her eyes. "We can see each other the following day."

Sam's here. Did that have anything to do with her not wanting to be with him? God, he *was* clingy.

"That's fine." He returned to Sam's bag and lifted it. "I'm going to make sure Sam is settled in."

"Yup." She turned back to the potatoes.

Something was up, but after pushing her so hard last

night, he didn't know if pushing her today would be a good idea. Penny had always bottled her emotions. It'd been difficult for her to be honest about her feelings. He wanted to respect that, but at times it drove him crazy.

"Your room is all set up and you can easily get to the family room from here." Luke paused in the doorway. Sam sat on the bed, holding his side. His face was crumpled in pain.

"What happened?" Luke dropped the bag and moved forward. He automatically reached for Sam's pulse.

"I just got winded." Sam took a shaky breath in. "You don't think they gave me a bum heart valve, do you?"

His pulse was fine. A little higher than Luke would like, but not in a danger zone. "You need to lie down for a bit and rest."

Luke kneeled and undid Sam's sneakers.

"I'm not a baby." Sam coughed and groaned.

"No, but you just had surgery, so lay off." Tossing the sneakers to the side, Luke helped lift Sam's legs onto the bed. "You have water on your nightstand and also a bell."

"A bell?" Sam looked over as if Luke had said a snake was over there.

"To ring when you need something."

"I can take care of myself."

"No. You can't. When you ring the bell, I'll come help you. Trust me, it's only temporary. Don't get used to it." Luke stood and put the curtains down to block some of the sunlight. "Rest."

"Whatever." Sam punched the pillow. He laid back and closed his eyes.

Luke started out of the room.

"Luke?"

"Do you need something?"

Sam didn't open his eyes. "Thanks."

Luke didn't hide his shock. "You're welcome."

Sam grunted and rolled to face away from the door.

Luke stared at his back. How long had it been since he'd had a conversation with Sam that wasn't just a status update? How long since they'd been honest with each other? Luke had never brought up Sam's betrayal, but it had eaten away at what had been left of their relationship.

Shaking his head, Luke left the door open a crack before returning to the kitchen. Perfectly at home, Penny moved around the kitchen to make dinner for him and Sam.

"Are you sure you won't eat with us?"

Penny stopped midreach for the salt in the cupboard. Her mouth opened as if she was going to say something, but then she closed it as if she'd changed her mind. She shook her head instead and grabbed the salt.

"No salt for Sam." Luke leaned on the counter next to the stove.

"Oh, right." She set the salt on the counter and stirred the pot. "That's about as spicy as I get with cooking, I'm afraid."

Luke crossed to the cabinet and pulled down a few dried herbs, which had probably been in there since his mother died. "Try these."

"Thank you."

He wanted to say more. He wanted to talk about Sam, but she seemed so distant. Was she already starting to push him away? Why, after letting him closer last night? It was a vicious cycle with Penny. Even in high school, one day she'd be warm and caring. The next she'd be cold and distant. He'd thought it was the birth control she'd been on, but maybe it'd been more her than he'd wanted to believe.

"Are you going to stare at me while I cook? Aren't there chores or something to be done?" Penny glanced over and flashed him a wicked smile. "Don't make me get inventive with this wooden spoon."

His chest loosened and he held up his hands in surrender. "I don't know what you have in mind, but something tells me I wouldn't like it. I'll go see if the pigs could use some cuddling."

Penny hadn't exactly lied about having work to do this morning, but she could have stayed longer last night if she wanted to. The problem was every time she was near Sam she felt sick to her stomach. She may not be overly discriminating with whom she went out with these days, but back then...

She picked up the small tea sets and placed them on her cart. Once a month she did a full cleaning of the store. Everything came off the shelf. She cleaned each and every piece and did an inventory. It took her about a week to get through the entire store, but it made the store smell less like old stuff and more clean and fresh, with just a hint of old-stuff smell for atmosphere.

The door jangled as someone entered. She set down her rag and wiped her hands on the towel.

"Hello?" she called out as she walked to the front of the store.

"Hello?" returned a male voice that seemed familiar.

"Can I help you?" She stopped when she saw him. Jasper Ballard stood at her door. All six-foot, well-built, hunky goodness of him. Dark hair and brown eyes and a dimple on his right cheek.

"Hey, I was passing through town..." He smiled that

lopsided smile of his that had always gotten her motor revving. But not this time.

She shook herself out of her shocked stillness and headed for the cash register and the desk that would separate her from him. "How long are you in town?"

Her actions seemed to confuse him. She was usually overly friendly when he made his jaunts through Tawnee Valley. The local eligible male population was sadly lacking and most of them didn't hold a candle to Jasper. Jasper wasn't exactly a migrant worker, but he went from place to place looking for farming work. She rarely saw him in the winter, but when he was in town, he definitely liked to hook up. Normally she was all for it, but this time, it was complicated.

"For a few weeks. Looking for some easy money." He leaned his hands against her desk.

"Easy? Right. Because working on a farm is a piece of cake."

"For me it is." He flexed his arms, showing her their strength. If possible he'd developed more muscle since the last time he'd been in town. "Can I see you while I'm in town?"

"Uh…" Penny didn't want to burn this particular bridge. He was easy on the eyes and good in bed. But right now, she didn't want anyone but Luke. But Luke wouldn't be around forever, and eventually she'd have an itch.

The bell above the door saved her from having to come up with some excuse without blowing him off entirely.

Her eyes went to the door. Her heart froze in her chest. Luke.

His gaze took in Jasper's form and his casual stance.

Then those blue eyes flowed over her. He noticed every detail, making her want to squirm under his scrutiny.

"Penny." He closed the distance between them and the air around her grew heavy. Luke stuck out his hand to Jasper. "Luke Ward, and you are?"

"Jasper Ballard." Jasper's gaze flicked to hers for a moment before returning to Luke. "You part of the Ward farm?"

"Yeah, my brother owns it."

"I was heading out there this afternoon." Jasper stood with his feet apart and his arms crossed. "Sam usually has some odds and ends this time of year that he uses my help on."

"Sam's sick," Penny interjected, though neither man looked her way.

"I'd be willing to come out and help. My next job is in a week or so, but I work hard and don't mess around," Jasper said. "You can ask Sam about me if you want his approval. Here's my card."

Luke took the card and flipped it over in his hand. "I'll have to check with Sam about the finances, but we could use some more manpower."

"Great. I'll come out later this afternoon to see if we can make this work." Jasper winked at Penny. "I'll see you later, gorgeous."

Before she could get out a not-right-now-thank-you, Jasper was out the door, leaving her alone with Luke. She busied herself with the little knickknacks on the counter as if her life depended on getting them exactly in line.

"We going to talk about this?" Luke placed his hand over hers.

Her gaze bounced up to his and then back down. "Talk about what?"

Ignorance would save her. From what…she didn't know. She hadn't done anything wrong. She hadn't even encouraged Jasper. She just hadn't gotten the chance to say she was taken for now. And now she'd have to find Jasper to let him know that it wasn't going to happen this time.

Luke placed the card in her line of sight. "Is this why you were busy last night?"

"No." She met his gaze square on. "Of course not. I haven't seen him in over a year until this morning. Here in the shop, where we most definitely did not have sex."

"But he was the last guy you had sex with?"

"If it's any of your business, yeah. So what?" She pulled her hand back and crossed her arms.

"Do you even know him?"

"What does it matter?"

"It matters who you sleep with."

"For the last time, I didn't sleep with him. We had sex and it was good sex. There's nothing wrong with that."

"Is that all we are?" Luke flipped the card over and put it in the back pocket of his jeans. "Sex?"

"Why?" Penny threw her hands up. "What does it matter whether what I feel for you is more than sex? What is it going to change? You hate me for what I did. You know that I sleep around. That my standards are pretty low, except when it comes to you."

She felt as if she were ripping her heart open and spilling it all over the counter, but she didn't care. "We were fine apart. I got to do my thing and you got to do yours. You were only supposed to be here for the weekend."

"I'm here and I'm glad that I am." He came around

the counter and rested his hands on her shoulders. "We left some things unfinished, unsaid."

She braced herself, waiting for the anger and the accusations. Even though she felt strong on the outside, her heart felt like a brutalized piece of meat.

"I don't know where we go from here. I don't even know where here is." His hands squeezed her shoulders. "You promised me you'd try. I promise you I'll try to trust you."

Her eyes widened. She put her hands on his chest. "Trust?"

How could he say that after what she'd done to him? Kissing his own brother. Betraying every ounce of trust they had in their relationship. Making him feel like an idiot for ever believing her over all those guys.

"Yeah." His smile softened. "If you say you aren't having sex with that guy, I'll believe you. Just promise me if you decide to sleep—have sex with that guy or anyone else, you'll give me a heads-up. That way I can convince you not to."

He brushed his lips against hers, and that little fizzle of warmth spread throughout her chilled body. "Why?"

"Why would I convince you? Because you're hot and I'm horny."

She pushed on his chest. "You know what I mean."

"Because, Penny..." He kissed her and hugged her close.

Giving in to her desire, she rested her head against his chest and breathed in the freshness of him. His arms could make anything better. The day a little brighter. She wished she could stay here all the time and never let him go. "Because?"

"Because you make me feel alive. I like the way I feel

with you. I tried to forget how you made me feel by putting hundreds of miles between us. Let me be enough for you. For as long as this lasts…let me be enough."

Chapter Twelve

The next few days flew by in a haze. Penny kept busy at the store during the day and Luke showed up every night, though only for a short period before he went back out to be with Sam. Their time together wasn't just about sex anymore. They talked about everything. Her store. His medical career. The crappy stuff he had to do out at the farm. The crazy tourist with the yappy dog she'd insisted on bringing into Penny's shop.

What they didn't talk about was the past. Or their feelings. Which was fine with Penny.

Today was her day off, so she decided to drive out to the farm to check on Sam, as she promised Amber. She also planned to clean the house because the men likely hadn't had time to with everything that had to be done on the farm.

Jasper and Luke waved from the field as she passed by to turn down the driveway. Jasper hadn't shown up at her doorstep yet. Maybe Luke had told him that she was unavailable. Or maybe Jasper had noticed Luke's car in her driveway. Either way she was glad it was a nonissue.

She parked and grabbed the bags of groceries out of the back. As she walked into the kitchen, the screen door slammed behind her. Someone had tightened the spring again.

She set the bags on the counter and started to unload them. It hadn't taken her long to figure out the kitchen setup when she'd been out here with Luke and Amber.

"Oh, it's you." Sam stood in the doorway with his perma-scowl on.

"Sorry to disappoint." Penny didn't look up from unloading groceries.

Sam walked into the kitchen and sat on one of the wooden chairs.

"Shouldn't you be in a comfy chair or your bed?"

Sam rested his head on his hands. "Not you, too. How many reruns and episodes of *Judge Judy* do you people think I can take?"

Penny shrugged and grabbed the empty bags to store in the closet. When she turned back, Sam was looking at her expectantly, so she asked him, "Did you need something to eat?"

"Sure." Sam brushed his hand over his jaw. "I'd do it myself, but I'm too feeble apparently."

Penny shook her head and smiled. "Dr. Luke has you on lockdown?"

Sam nodded miserably.

"One grilled cheese sandwich coming up." She got out the bread, cheese and margarine and started heating up a skillet. She wasn't used to being alone with Sam.

His silence had always been somewhat off-putting to her; she liked to talk.

"Amber called me yesterday." Sam's voice shattered the silence.

"How's she doing?" Penny buttered the bread and unwrapped the cheese. Sam must be really bored if he was willing to talk to her.

"She's having the time of her life and trying not to sound like it."

Penny glanced back in time to catch Sam's smile. Weird.

He pulled out a farm magazine and flipped through the pages.

"I've talked to her every day, and she's always excited about all the rides. So..." Penny crossed her arms over her chest. "What's your secret?"

"What?" He stopped flipping and looked up at her.

"Before you came along, I was Amber's favorite person to hang out with. We'd order pizza, do our nails and watch romantic tween movies together." She waved the spatula at him. "Did you bribe her with chocolate? Or is it the dogs? Because I got her one of those, too."

Sam scratched his chin. "I don't know. I give her chores and she asks for more. Maybe it's because I don't treat her like a kid."

Penny narrowed her eyes. "Are you sure it isn't chocolate? Because I can totally hook her up with chocolate."

"She likes the animals." Sam shrugged.

"I'm not about to install a circus in my backyard." She turned and put his sandwich in the skillet.

"Guess you won't win, then."

She spun around, but he had his head buried in the magazine again. "I wouldn't taunt the woman making your meal, Sam Ward."

"It can't taste any worse than my cooking, no matter what you do to it."

Penny laughed and turned back to the stove. "Luke used to always try to eat at my place or we'd go out somewhere. He said he'd starve to death if he had to live on what you prepared."

"I haven't starved yet."

She finished his sandwich and put it on a plate. She grabbed a diet pop and some carrots from the fridge and placed it all in front of Sam.

"Thanks."

"No problem." Penny washed the pan and the spatula and put them in the drying rack. She scrubbed down the counters and the rest of the kitchen while Sam ate his lunch and read the magazines.

"How was the sandwich?" she asked as she took his empty plate.

"Pretty good." Sam glanced up at her. "But we already know I have the taste buds of a dog."

"True." Penny smiled.

The screen door creaked as it was pulled open. They both looked toward the door as Luke came in. He stopped and the door slammed shut behind him.

His mouth opened and closed. Penny realized how close she was standing to Sam's chair and stepped back. Jasper followed Luke in.

"Penny! Long time no see." Jasper winked, completely oblivious to the tension in the room. The door slammed behind him. "What's for lunch?"

"I think I'm going to go lie down." Sam rose from his chair and headed back toward his bedroom.

Penny went to the sink and washed the plate in the water she had left from doing the pan. She'd done nothing wrong, but her stomach rolled and pitched like a boat caught in a storm.

"Guess I'll get my own lunch. You want anything, Luke?" Jasper said.

"Nah, I'm good. I think I'll go wash up some."

She knew the moment he left the room. Some of the warmth left with him.

"So you and Luke, eh?" Jasper said as he sat at the table. "I guess that means I'll have to find another lovely companion to spend my time with in Tawnee Valley."

She set the dish in the drying rack and faced Jasper. "I'm sure you'll have no trouble securing a 'companion.'"

"I don't know about that." He took a drink from his pop can. "Most of the women are looking for someone to marry them so they can pop out a few brats. Or someone to take care of the brats they already have."

"That sounds pretty bitter." She leaned against the counter and crossed her arms. "Harboring some resentment there?"

"Hardly. I just know the lay of the land. The young ones are looking for a way to get out of town. The older ones are looking for someone to hold on to." Jasper smiled. "You are definitely one of a kind."

"How so?"

"You don't want anything from guys except sex. No strings. No attachment. No having to fake I care. You get yours and I get mine and we go on our separate ways."

The way he described it, sex with her was a transaction. She'd never put much thought into it. It was a basic need like eating and sleeping. Lots of people attached significance to the act that she just didn't.

Luke walked in and she met his gaze.

Except with Luke. It was more than sex with him. Her breath caught in her throat and her knees felt as if they were going to give out from underneath her. She'd tried to keep that distance she needed, but somehow she'd fallen for him.

She loved him. It hit her like a punch to the gut. Her heart had always belonged to him, but part of her had always held itself apart. The part that knew no matter how hard she tried to stay with him, it wouldn't last. Love? She fought against the realization…and the need to breathe.

He was going to leave soon and she wouldn't be able to do anything about it. Her heart collapsed in her chest.

"Are you okay?" Concern filled Luke's blue eyes as he crossed the kitchen. He rubbed her arms.

Her head felt light and darkness surrounded her.

"Penny. Breathe."

She gasped in air.

The world spun as Luke swept her up in his arms. She linked her hands behind his head, more by instinct than by conscious thought.

"Keep breathing," he said quietly as he carried her up the stairs and into his bedroom. He kicked the door shut behind him and laid her on the bed. Sitting next to her, he brushed his hand over her forehead and her hair. "Tell me what's wrong."

I love you—that's what's wrong. Heat rushed to her cheeks. "I just got faint, is all."

"Has this happened before?" He took her wrist in his hand and watched his watch as he took her pulse.

"No." Only once. Even though she'd done it intentionally…. When she'd realized what she'd done with Sam. When she realized that everything she'd wanted was never to be hers. Because the only thing she had ever really wanted was Luke.

She'd never questioned her decision. It had been for the best. They couldn't possibly last because love didn't last. At least not for her. At some point everyone she loved went away.

Taking deep breaths, she tried to slow down her racing heart. "I'm feeling better now."

When she tried to sit, Luke gently pushed her shoulder back to the bed. "I shouldn't come over every night. You have work. You need rest."

She shook her head. She'd never needed much sleep, and having Luke was worth needing to down an extra cup of coffee in the morning. "I get plenty of sleep."

"Maybe we should cool it for a night."

She grabbed his hand. She didn't want to miss a single day with him. All too soon he'd be gone and she'd be alone. He might not have moved on yet, but he would. Luke was built for happily ever after. Just not with her.

"Luke, we don't need to cool it. I'm getting enough sleep. It was probably just the heat in the kitchen." She grasped at straws.

He brushed the hair off her forehead and smiled. "It's okay. Tonight you get some sleep and tomorrow night we'll go out on a real date. With dinner and a movie and all that crap."

She relaxed into the bed and grabbed his hand. Tracing his fingers with her fingertip, she said, "That sounds great, but you should still come over tonight."

Time alone was something she didn't need. She would have plenty of time alone after he left. She wanted the oblivion making love with him gave her. She needed it.

He leaned down and kissed her. Slow and steady. It

wasn't earth-shattering, but it was everything to her. It was the pleasure she would remember when winter came and she had to cuddle with the dog to keep warm.

Luke lifted his head. "Maybe if you are good, I'll try to make it by."

She gave a dramatic sigh and held her arm over her eyes. "Then I'm doomed because I'm never good."

"You're always good to me, Penny."

She peeked out from behind her arm. "You're the good one."

He stood and pulled her up gently, checking her eyes closely while he pulled her to sitting and then to standing. She squinted back at him.

"I'm fine, Luke." Just terminally in love.

Chapter Thirteen

Penny pulled the blanket around herself, and Flicker snuggled closer to her. The television volume was low enough that she would hear Luke's knock on her door. When she'd left the farm earlier, he'd given her a scorching kiss that felt more like a promise than a good-night kiss.

Fortunately, *My Best Friend's Wedding* was on cable to keep her occupied while she waited. Sleep was the last thing on her mind. She had to deal with the fact that she was in love with Luke, but she had pushed him away long ago by kissing Sam. Seeing that had been brutal enough to keep Luke away for years.

It hadn't hurt only Luke, though. He'd left her without asking for an explanation. Just assumed the worst and left, as she'd known he would. Luke had never been the jealous type. At least not when they were teenagers. He had been so confident in their love. And he had every reason to be. She had loved him with everything she had. But the thought of trying to make it in the real world—outside of the bubble of Tawnee Valley—had brought back memories of her mother.

She glanced at the time. If he didn't show up in the next thirty minutes, she would text him. She'd make up some excuse, like she was feeling faint and needed a doctor. He would show up and take her in his arms and make her feel alive.

But for how long? Could she really let him go again? Even if it would be better for both of them? He had his job at the hospital and she had her store. Three hundred miles apart. This was the one time that their lives had intersected in almost nine years. That definitely didn't boost her confidence that this could actually work.

She tried to concentrate on the story line of the movie. The future would come quickly enough without her worrying over it.

Just as she was dozing off, there was a knock at the door. Flicker lifted his head and then lay back down.

"My ferocious guard dog." Penny shook her head as she walked to the front door. Maybe she should make Luke a key. That way even if she did fall asleep he could come in and wake her up. That put a smile on her face.

"I was beginning to think you wouldn't show up." She yanked open the door and her heart plummeted. Instead of Luke on her porch, a woman about her height stood in the shadows.

Apprehension filled her as Penny flicked on the porch light. A ghost would have made more sense than what she was seeing.

"Hi, baby," Cheryl Montgomery said. Her auburn hair was streaked with silver. Her familiar brown eyes were so light they were almost tan. Her build was similar to Penny's, but her clothes were loose around her small frame. Even though it had been over fifteen years since Penny had last seen her, she would always recognize her mother.

That didn't mean that she could handle it. Her brain went completely blank trying to process this unexpected arrival. She couldn't think, let alone speak. Her chest burned as if she'd run for miles without stopping. Her hands were cold and clammy.

"Are you going to invite me in?" Cheryl looked around Penny into the house and smiled hesitantly. "From what I see you've changed some things since Mom died."

"You didn't come to the funeral." It was her voice, but Penny hadn't realized she'd said anything. She'd had seventeen years to come up with something to say when her mother finally showed up, but she'd never believed it would actually happen.

Cheryl looked down at her feet before lifting her gaze to Penny. "Do we have to talk about this on the porch? It's kind of chilly."

She didn't want her mother in this house. It was hers now. Anything she'd had as a child, her mother had destroyed, whether she'd sold it so she could buy more liquor or she'd broken it during one of her alcohol-induced rampages. Penny had never had anything until her grandma took her in. The few treasures her grandma had given her were on the dresser in her bedroom.

"I swear I'm sober." Cheryl held up a coin. "One year."

Penny wanted to scream and slam the door in Cheryl's face. Instead she stepped aside and let her in. Blood thundered in her ears as she followed her mother into her living room.

"This is so much better than my mother's decorations. She never did like much color." Cheryl moved to the wall of photos. "Is this your daughter?"

"No, I don't have any children." Penny stood next to the door frame with her arms crossed in front of her.

"That's a shame. She's a pretty girl. I'd love to be a grandma."

Don't hold your breath on that one, Mom. Cheryl would likely be the worst grandma in the world. She had definitely never received a Number One Mom mug from Penny.

Cheryl sat in the recliner and looked at Penny expectantly.

There was no way Penny was going to sit down and talk as if nothing had happened with the woman who had abandoned her. As if this was some kind of happy reunion between mother and daughter. As if she hadn't waited for her for seventeen years. "Why weren't you at Grandma's funeral?"

Cheryl sighed and clasped her hands in her lap. "I got into some trouble and had to go into rehab."

"The funeral was four years ago. You just said you've only been sober a year." It was hard to keep the accusation out of her voice. Penny didn't want her mother to matter to her. She didn't want anything to do with Cheryl at all.

"I relapsed, but I went into the program myself afterward."

"Who'd you end up in bed with?" Penny tried to keep the venom from her voice.

Cheryl lowered her eyes and took a deep breath. "You have every right to be mad at me, Penny—"

"Really? For what, *Cheryl?* Making me clean up your vomit after you'd partied all night? Or how about how I'd have to skip school to take care of you when you were hungover? Or how about the sleazy men you brought into my life? Thank God you had the decency to give me a bolt on my bedroom door. The handle rattled enough to make me fear going to the bathroom at night because you'd be too passed out to actually help me."

"I wasn't a good mom. I wasn't a good anything." Cheryl lifted her gaze to Penny. "I want to make this right. I want to start fresh. I want to be a family."

Penny recoiled as if her mother had asked her to join a cult that worshiped goats and sacrificed bunnies for fun. "What about what I wanted, Cheryl?"

She'd begged her mother not to leave her behind. When they'd lived together, she'd reached out for help for her mother's addiction and every now and then, Cheryl would clean up and they'd be happy. Until Cheryl let another man into her life, and it wasn't long after that the drinking would begin again. Even though Penny had hated cleaning up her mother's mess, she hadn't wanted to leave her. And she'd never thought that Cheryl would leave her behind.

I love you, Penny. We'll be together soon. I just need to fix myself right now. The words had echoed in her head for years while she waited for her mother to come get her and for them to be a family again.

"I…" Cheryl looked confused. She flipped the coin over in her hand and closed her eyes. Taking a deep breath, she raised her gaze to Penny. "I can't take back the past. All I can do is apologize and try to make you believe that I never wanted to leave you."

Penny's lips tightened to a thin line. That was the one thing she would never believe. She stared at Cheryl and wondered what lies would come out of her mouth next.

Cheryl frowned and put the coin in her pocket. "I

don't know what else I can say. I'm late, but Alan says better late than never. So here I am."

"Alan," Penny spit out the name. "Is that the most recent in your train wreck of boyfriends?"

She shook her head. "He's my sponsor. He's been sober for fifteen years. He's happily remarried with kids."

"Good for him." Everything inside Penny wanted to explode. This wasn't happening. It was some sort of sick joke. Why was *she* here after everything? Where had *she* been when Penny had needed her?

They stared at each other, and Cheryl's eyes pleaded with her to understand. To forgive. But that wasn't in Penny. She couldn't just forget. Not when it had cost her everything.

The knock on the door broke their gazes. Penny took a deep breath and released it as she turned to go answer the door.

"Hey, I brought you—" Luke looked up from the bag he held. "What's wrong?"

She could feel the sob pressing on her throat. She wanted to hug him and let go of everything, but she didn't. Luke would save her because that's what he did.

"My mom is here." The words came out flat. She couldn't put any emotion behind them or she wouldn't make it through the next few minutes. *Just hold it together for a few more minutes.* That's all she needed.

Luke closed her door and set the bag down on the table. Then he took her hand in his. It was all things good and warm. She drew strength from him. He would be here for her and that meant the world to her.

She led him back to the living room. Cheryl looked expectantly at Penny and then over to Luke.

"Hello, Ms. Montgomery. I'm Luke Ward." He didn't

release Penny's hand to offer to shake Cheryl's. He stood with her as a united front.

Penny wanted to lean into him, let him take care of this situation, but she hadn't grown into a wet mop at the sight of her mother. She wasn't going to start acting like one now because Luke was here.

"It's nice to meet you, Luke." Cheryl stood. "I didn't realize Penny was expecting company."

Penny couldn't think of anything to say. She wanted her mother to leave, but that part of her that had taken care of her mother reared up. "Do you have some place to go?"

For a moment, she thought her mother was going to ask to stay with her. Luke squeezed her hand and she realized she had him in a death grip and loosened it slightly.

"I've got a room in Owen. I didn't want to assume that you would forgive me right away." She laughed awkwardly. "I hoped, but…"

Penny's heart felt as if it had been through a blender today. She shook her head as the tears pressed against the back of her eyes.

"I didn't think so." Cheryl took in a deep breath and held her head up. "I hope that you'll let me come and see you."

Penny didn't say anything but stepped out of the way so that Cheryl could leave.

Cheryl sighed and walked to the door. Once there, she stopped and turned back. "I know you don't believe me, but I love you, Penny."

Penny had never doubted that. She just wasn't enough for her mother.

"Good night, Luke."

"Good night, Ms. Montgomery."

"You can call me Cheryl." She smiled wearily. "Penny does."

With that she was gone. As soon as the door closed, Penny collapsed against Luke.

Chapter Fourteen

It had to be a cosmic joke. Penny could take only so much. Luke folded her in his arms against his chest, and she allowed the first choking sob to escape.

Her whole world had just been shaken. The pain she'd felt when her mother had left her resurfaced. How many nights had she cried herself to sleep in her bedroom? How many times had she sworn her mother would come tomorrow? How many nights had she re-packed her suitcase?

Until one day she just knew. Her mother would never come back for her. Just as her father had never wanted her. What had made her believe her mother was any different than him? Just because she was the one who got stuck with Penny? Sure, she'd said she loved Penny. But love was a deception.

"Do you want to go sit down?" Luke ran his hands over her back and brushed her hair away from her face.

"Why are you so good to me?" Penny looked up at him through the tears gathering in her eyes.

He smiled softly and kissed her forehead. "Because someone has to be good to you. It might as well be me."

Penny backed away out of his arms. She needed to give him something. Something important to her. Taking his hand, she pulled him behind her up the stairs and down the hallway. At the door to her bedroom, she stopped and turned to face him.

"This doesn't mean anything." She said the words but knew they weren't true. This was the one rule she'd held close all these years. If no one came into her bedroom, she'd be safe. She wouldn't have memories, except of herself, attached to the one place in her world that was hers. If she let Luke in, every time she entered her bedroom she'd think of him in it. Somehow forever seemed bearable when it came to Luke.

She searched his eyes for a long minute. It wouldn't matter if she looked into them for hours; she wouldn't know how to find what she was looking for, because she didn't know what it looked like. At least not as other people did. Love.

Pushing the door open behind her, she pulled him into her bedroom. As he closed the door, her heart shuddered. This was as close as she might ever come to telling Luke she loved him. The words weren't possible. Not when this all would end. She couldn't reopen that wound, but she could show him how she felt.

Her room wasn't much. Bed, dresser, lamp, nightstand. But her treasures sat arranged on a white doily on her dresser. Everything in here was hers and hers alone. No one could take them from her.

She dropped his hand and walked to her queen-size bed. Sitting down with her back against the headrest, she propped up a few pillows beside her and patted the bed. Not saying a word, Luke kicked off his shoes and joined her. Side by side.

Deep breaths. She took his hand in hers, leaned against his shoulder and let out a long sigh.

"You want to talk about it?" Luke rubbed his thumb across her knuckles.

Penny shook her head. "You don't want to hear about it."

"Don't hide yourself from me, Penny." Luke tipped her chin up and gazed into her eyes. "I care about you, and I know that had to have been painful."

She wanted to deny it. To press her body against his and take his mouth with hers until they both forgot about Cheryl's visit. But she couldn't. Her mother's visit had unlocked a dam that had been ready to burst for years.

"She left me when I was ten."

Years ago, she'd told Luke some of the story, but she wanted to get it all out now. As he listened, he held her hand in his and kept rubbing his thumb across her knuckles. His touch gave her comfort and courage.

"Sometimes it was good. It would be me and her against the world. She was fun and a little crazy. We moved a lot. Wherever she could find work. When she first started a job, we'd have a little extra money. She'd buy me gifts and ice cream. I'd go to school like a normal kid."

She closed her eyes as she rested against his shoulder. Remembering the good times was almost more painful than remembering the bad. Without the good, she would have never known that the other times were that bad.

"We'd spend the weekends like a normal family. I'd join the basketball team at school. Then mom would find a guy. She never really stopped drinking, just drank less during the good times. Things would start to get rough and she'd start drinking more. He'd get sick of her and she'd find herself at the bottom of a bottle."

"That couldn't have been easy for you." Luke put his arm around her and took her hand with his other.

"She'd start getting sick. I'd have to clean up after her just so I could use the bathroom. I'd miss school to stay home to take care of her and make sure she ate and was hydrated. She'd always go right back to the bottle, though, and bring home any guy who would have her."

A shudder ran through her. "I'd lock myself in my room those nights. But I'd always be there in the morning to help her. I thought that's what love was. Always being there. No matter what."

She shook her head. "She'd lose her job and then she'd start selling things to get more alcohol. Everything she'd bought me would be gone within a few days. I'd use any spare money I could find to get us food. Sometimes we only had ramen noodles all week. I cooked. I cleaned. When I was exhausted, I'd reach out for help."

"You were brave."

"Not brave. Scared." She struggled to form the next part into words. "It wasn't that I couldn't take care of her anymore. It was that I couldn't control her anymore. When we had no money left to buy food, I worried that she'd have to start selling herself to maintain her addiction. When she drank heavily, she wasn't my mom anymore. She didn't care about me. When she'd sober up, she'd apologize. She'd swear she wouldn't drink anymore. She'd go out to find a job and then come home drunk."

She swiped at the tear that had escaped down her cheek. "But I could handle it. I knew she loved me and I was there for her. It was us against everything. I looked into rehab, but every place wanted her to stay for a long time to get clean. How was I supposed to survive without my mom? They would have thrown me into foster care."

"What about your grandma?"

Penny scoffed. "Grandma threw out Mom when she found out she was pregnant. You remember how strict Grandma had been with me?"

She felt his nod against her head.

"She was that way because Mom had run wild. Not that I didn't, but Mom had started drinking at fourteen. Grandma had told Mom never to come to her for anything. She'd broken the rules and that was that. Grandma didn't care what Mom had to do to survive.

"So we had no one but each other. For years we made it work. I don't know what changed. I thought about it for a long time. Had she gotten sick of me? Had I done something wrong? I was always helpful. I might have talked back a few times, but that wasn't anything new."

Penny struggled to sit up straight and put a little distance between her and Luke, but she didn't let go of his hand. "When she brought me to my grandma, I begged her not to leave me. What would she do without me to take care of her? How would she remember to eat?"

Luke squeezed her hand. "Maybe she just wanted you to have someone to look out for you for a change."

"By leaving me with Grandma? By taking away everything I'd ever known?" Penny blinked away the tears. "She was supposed to come back. She promised. She said—"

Tears choked her and she couldn't hold them back anymore. Luke pulled her toward him and she fell against his chest, soaking his blue T-shirt with her tears. He gently stroked her hair and made soothing noises.

For seventeen years she'd held it inside. Pushed it down deep so that it wouldn't consume her. Forced everyone in her life away. Grandma had been easy. She had always kept Penny at arm's length. Penny had been just another thing she had to take care of, not a grandchild to be loved and cherished. It had probably been better that way. Penny would have pushed back hard if her grandma had wanted any sort of real relationship with her.

"She left me with my grandma. All alone. Maggie and I got to be friends, but for years I could never really make it real because I thought that someday Mom would come back for me. And we'd leave Tawnee Valley and start our lives together. But she never came...."

His warmth penetrated the coldness that had engulfed her when she'd seen her mother. But she still shook as the tears streamed down her cheeks.

"How could she leave me if she loved me?"

Chapter Fifteen

Luke held Penny as she released what had to be years of pent-up emotion. As the sobs diminished, he could feel her body relaxing against his, until her breath became even and slow. He grabbed a tissue from the nightstand and patted her face dry as she slept.

Everyone knew that Cheryl Montgomery had dropped her daughter at her mother's and run off. A few people remembered she'd had issues with alcohol in high school. Before Penny had been at school a month, most of their classmates had labeled her a lost cause. Probably because their parents didn't want a bad influence around them. But Penny hadn't been bad. Not at first.

After a while she seemed to become whatever they thought she should become. He wished he'd been strong enough to turn the tide. To make his classmates and the people they grew up with forget their prejudice. But he hadn't.

Of course, at the time he had a mom and dad who loved their children and who would do anything for them.

Luke slipped his cell phone out of his jeans. He texted Jasper that he'd be back later than he'd planned and asked him to look in on Sam. Jasper texted back, No problem. Luke set the phone on the nightstand and settled down further on the bed, keeping Penny close.

She was the puzzle he could spend the rest of his life solving. Even Jasper made sense once Luke got over his initial jealousy. It still bugged him that Penny had used Jasper to scratch an itch, but part of him was glad it had been Jasper, a loner without an attachment to anywhere or anyone. He would never have tried to settle down and be the man that Penny needed in her life.

Maybe *needed* wasn't the right term. Luke stroked her hair. Because any man who loved Penny would have to love her unconditionally and forgive her, knowing that something truly wild would never be true to one person.

Perhaps he should turn in his man card because of all the gushy stuff going through his mind. The thing was, as much as he wanted to be that man for Penny, he wasn't sure he could forgive her for Sam. Anyone else, yes…but Sam?

"Don't you need to go home?" Penny's voice was sleepy. She didn't even open her eyes, just stayed where she was across his chest.

"I'm good here." Because home had always been with Penny. Over the years, he'd thought of her and what she would say about what he was doing. She wasn't his moral compass—she'd always had a skewed perspective for whatever she wanted. But sometimes being a little selfish instead of selfless was just what the doctor ordered.

And right now, he wanted to be in this bed with this woman. Until she kicked him out. He closed his eyes and focused on the rhythm of her breathing.

Her eyes felt like grit paper when Penny tried to open them. They felt swollen and her chest still ached slightly. Even opening her eyes didn't help much; the room was dark. Her alarm clock read 4:24 a.m.

Luke's warm body was the only thing keeping the chill of the room from making her shiver and dive under the covers. She pressed in closer and breathed him in.

"You keep doing that and I won't be responsible for my actions." Luke's voice was low and rough.

"Thank you for listening to me," she whispered. With the darkness surrounding them, it felt safe to admit she'd needed him.

"Thank you for letting me in." He hugged her to him.

She slid off him and onto the mattress. He turned on his side to face her. Just enough light from the streetlights peeked through the curtain to let her make out his features. Her heart swelled in her chest. She wanted to tell him everything, from how stupid she had been to push him away to how much she was falling for him again.

Instead she leaned in and kissed him. Gently, exploring with just a hint of the raw passion that normally devoured them. He followed her lead, seeming to know that this time wasn't so much about fulfilling a desire but exploring the connection they shared.

His hand settled on her waist and sent intense waves of longing through her. Longing to stay in his arms forever. To be one with him. Things she'd never have, but tonight she'd cling to them and let herself dream of a future where they could be together.

"You're shaking," Luke said as he trailed kisses from her mouth to her throat. "We should get you under the covers."

"I'm not cold." Her eyes fluttered shut as his hand trailed across her belly.

"Good." He plucked the bottom button of her shirt undone.

Her breath caught and he flicked another button open. When she opened her eyes, he was watching her face. Another button and his knuckles brushed against her bare skin. Her stomach tightened and a burst of heat sparked through her system.

She reached up and ran her hand along his scruffy jaw. His cheek twitched under her fingertips. One more button loosened. She ran her fingers through his hair and brought his mouth down to hers. Kissing Luke was like Christmas and her birthday rolled into one. Excitement, anticipation, joy.

His fingertips grazed the underside of her breast and she gasped. Even though they had been more intimate previously, tonight felt like the start of something new. Or maybe it was the end of everything they had. She brushed off the dark thought and let herself be in this moment, no matter the consequence.

Her heart was already his. It always had been. It always would be. But it wasn't just her heart she was giving to him. As he undid the remaining buttons and opened her shirt, he gazed down at her silhouette. His fingers were rough from helping out at the farm as they trailed down over her white lace bra and across her stomach down to the waistband of her dark slacks.

Normally she'd be helping him remove her clothes

and his, but something about the quiet house, her bedroom and the darkness, this man, made her want to take things slowly. Luke kissed along the lace edge of her bra, making her nipples harden and beg for his touch.

He lifted his head and kissed her mouth as his hand traced along the band of her bra, then unhooked it in the back.

"I've never met anyone who ties me up in knots the way you do," he said before pushing her shirt off her shoulders. He nipped at every inch of her skin he exposed until her breath and pulse pounded.

She wanted to come back with something to take away the seriousness. But when he pulled off her shirt and slowly eased off her bra, her mouth went dry. His lips closed around her nipple. Any thought she might have had was gone in the flash fire of desire that seared through her.

Helpless to the heat flooding her, she held on to him as he took his time to explore one breast and then the other. If she bound him in ropes, he held her in chains. Surely ropes would break, whereas her chains would hold her to him forever.

Love wasn't a blessing to Penny. It was a curse that bound her to a mother who easily cast her off when she became too much of a burden and to a man who had been easily dissuaded from his pursuit. It didn't stop her from loving him or wanting to be loved by him.

When his mouth found hers again, she wished she could be more aloof and brush him off. But she couldn't. Luke had been her rock and stability in high school. They'd turned each other away from self-destruction.

His touch had always wiped away the bad. She hadn't been looking for a relationship the night at the dance when she'd approached him. With her reputation and his, she thought maybe they could raise a little hell. Instead they'd made each other better. Sure they'd done some crazy things, but he'd stopped picking fights and getting in trouble at school and she'd stopped trying to become her mother with booze and guys.

"Luke?" she said when he lifted his head.

He brushed the hair away from her face and brushed his thumb across her bottom lip. "Yeah?"

Tears pressed against her eyes. "Do you think I'm a bad person?"

"Never in a million years." He rested his head against his hand and looked down at her. "How can you think you're bad? You helped your best friend through her mother's death and helped her with her child. You took care of your mother when she needed you most. You helped your grandma and improved on her dream after she passed."

A tear slid free.

"But most of all you turned around a screwed-up teenager. Showed him what it was to be loved and how to fix his life instead of wreck it. You might want people to stay away and think that you are bad, but you are incredible." His hand reached down to her slacks and slowly undid the button and zipper.

"I never deserved you," she whispered. Her fingers played with the ends of his hair, caressing the softness.

He smiled and finished undressing her. His gaze followed her body from head to toe. The attention made her want to stretch like a cat and let him pet her until she purred.

He stood to take off his clothes. She tried to fill her head with memories for when he was gone. Tried to imagine what her life would be like once he was back in St. Louis. She couldn't begin to picture it without feeling her gut roll in protest.

Instead she held out her arms to him and drew him down to the bed. Sex would never be the same with anyone else. Just the feel of his skin against hers made her shiver with need. His kiss could steal her breath and bring her life. His hands kindled fire inside her everywhere they touched. His mouth on her skin made her melt.

No one had ever had the ability to make her burn with desire the way Luke did. She couldn't deny that what they were doing was making love. It was too intense, too emotional to be sex. He made her his and she couldn't resist.

When he entered her, she was so beyond herself that she raked her nails over his shoulders, trying to draw him closer.

He brushed her lips with his and whispered next to her ear, "Let go, Penny. Just let us be."

He moved slowly in her, building the already-raging fire into a blaze until he started to lose control and his breathing grew more ragged and his motions more intentional. Their bodies moved together, striving for release.

The edge was so near. Penny opened her eyes. Luke's face was twisted in pleasurable agony. She never wanted this to end, but she couldn't hold back any longer. Her release pulsed through her and it pushed him over.

I love you so much and you'll never know. The words rang through her mind as she slipped back into sleep.

Chapter Sixteen

Luke tried to concentrate on moving the bales of hay in the barn, but it didn't actually require brainpower, so his mind kept drifting back to Penny. How desperately she'd clung to his hand when introducing him to her mother. How vulnerable she'd been when she'd led him back to her room. How sensual she'd been lying beneath him.

"Watch out."

A bale of hay came flying down to land beside Luke. He looked up at Jasper in the rafter.

"What the hell?" Luke grabbed the bale by the strings and stacked it with the others. "You're lucky that didn't bust my head open."

"At least Penny would be available." Jasper smiled.

Luke grunted in response. The fact that Jasper still had a job out here meant Luke knew the man was teasing, but it didn't help that when he went back to

St. Louis in a few days Penny would be free to resume all her extracurricular activities.

He had no hold over Penny. She was as free as when he'd first seen her at the wedding. When he left, he would have no right to expect her to wait for him. When he left...

"Hey, I don't mind babysitting your brother so you can get some, but could you keep working so I can get out of here and hit the bars? Since you took the only hottie in town, I'm going to have to go trolling." Jasper swung down from the loft and landed a few feet from Luke.

This wasn't the first time Luke had the urge to knock the guy's smile in. Sam had insisted that Jasper would be an asset. But he'd also been an asset to Penny, which rubbed Luke the wrong way. If Penny had feelings for this guy, though, she would have said something. Wouldn't she have?

"Don't worry. You'll have plenty of time to get to the bar." Luke wiped the sweat from his forehead with a rag.

Besides, it hadn't been Jasper at her door last night and there for her when she needed someone to hold on to. She'd made a big fuss over never having anyone in her bed and never "sleeping" with anyone. Last night he'd been privy to both.

That had to count for something.

Luke climbed out of the barn and took off his work gloves. The sun was almost to midday. His skin itched from the hay and dust that clung to his sweat. He'd give his left nut for a shower, but that meant dealing with Sam.

He squinted up at the sun. It was starting to get too hot to do much, but staying outside seemed like the best defense against Sam, who couldn't seem to accept the fact that he needed to sit down and relax.

Even the dogs were napping in the shade. A drop of sweat rolled down his spine. It couldn't be helped. Luke needed a shower and everything else would have to wait until it got cooler.

"I'm heading to the house," Luke shouted back to Jasper.

"I'll take lunch after I finish this."

Taking a deep breath, Luke headed to the porch. The door creaked open and banged shut behind him. He swore.

Yesterday, Luke had readjusted the tension on the door so that it wouldn't bang shut anymore. Apparently Sam was using it as a way to know when someone was in the house and had reset it when Luke wasn't looking. Luke didn't know whether to be mad that Sam had adjusted the door or mad that he'd obviously not been sitting while he did it.

"Hey." Sam appeared in the doorway as Luke took off his shoes.

"Go lie down." Luke hung up the hat he'd been wearing. It hadn't helped to keep the hay from making his head itch.

"You guys got the bales out of the rafters?"

"Yeah." Luke had dusted off what he could outside, but hay clung stubbornly to his jeans. His dad would have dumped his jeans at the door; otherwise Mom would have yelled at him. The memory of his parents brought a bittersweet smile to his face.

"It's time to change the oil in the tractor," Sam said.

"I know." Luke glared at Sam. "You told me this morning and yesterday evening and yesterday morning."

"If it doesn't get done, you won't be able to get to the fields this afternoon." Sam's mouth was set in a stubborn line.

"I don't need to be micromanaged, Sam. I've got it covered." Luke brushed past Sam into the dining room. "Right now I need to get the hay off my skin. Unless you want to tell me how to do that, too."

"I'm sure you can handle that." Sam shuffled toward the living room.

Luke bit back anything he might have said. Sam was just trying to control a situation he felt was out of his control. It was one of the reasons he and Sam had butted heads as teenagers. It hadn't made sense to him that Sam had the right to give him punishments, but no one had been punishing Sam when he screwed up.

Sam had always been his father's favorite and got most of his attention. First Sam, then Brady, then Luke. Luke had been their mother's favorite, though. She'd always sneak him an extra cookie...for him to grow on.

He blinked back tears as he went into the bathroom. Penny's relationship with her mother was complicated— to put it mildly. But if Luke could see his mother one more time...he'd do whatever it would take.

He stripped and showered quickly before changing into fresh jeans and a T-shirt. It had been a while since he'd done so much manual labor, and sitting on his bed even long enough to pull socks on made him want to shut his eyes for a little while.

Maybe sleep would help him figure out what to do about Penny and Sam. She couldn't be trusted before. Had she really changed any? Sam hadn't changed. He was just as controlling. Just as stubborn.

Just a few minutes of sleep...

* * *

The bell above the door startled Penny into almost dropping the glass perfume bottle. Her head whipped around to see who had come in.

"Don't worry, dear. It's just me."

Penny didn't think she'd ever be relieved to see Bitsy Clemons coming through the door, but she was grateful it wasn't Cheryl, who was somewhere out there, lurking, and wanted a relationship with her. That had her on edge. That and Luke.... God, she'd been stupid last night. Wanting to cling to him as if he could ever love her again after what she did to him. She wouldn't blame him for never trusting her. But she'd wanted to believe for a few seconds that he could love her. Even if nothing came of it.

"I heard that your mother is staying in Owen." Bitsy's voice had a hint of a question at the end.

Penny decided to take it as a comment and not a question. She didn't want to acknowledge her mother's presence. She didn't want any part of the woman.

Bitsy rounded the corner and picked up a trinket off the shelf. "You wouldn't know anything about that, would you?"

Penny took in a deep breath and released it. "Yes. She came by the house last night."

Bitsy tsked and placed her hand on Penny's arm. "How are you holding up, dear?"

"I'm fine." Penny walked farther down the aisle.

"It's okay if you don't like the woman. After all, she all but left you with your grandmother—God rest her soul. You know we'll stand behind you. No matter what your decision regarding your mother."

Penny turned and looked into the serene face of Bitsy Clemons. "What do you mean?"

Bitsy smiled slightly, as if she had a secret to pass on. "Well, you didn't hear it from me, but word is Cheryl is looking at a few houses today in Tawnee Valley. Not to buy, of course, but to rent. A full-year lease."

Penny's heart clattered to a stop. "A year?"

"The Brindells' place over on First Street and the Adams' place over on Oak." Bitsy pretended to be interested in the shelf, but Penny could tell she was watching her like a hawk for the slightest reaction.

"What she does doesn't concern me." Penny straightened. "If she wants to be in our town, that's fine."

But it wasn't fine. It was terrifying, but if Bitsy saw even a hint of that, she'd tell everyone. Better to hold it in than to let the whole town know.

Cheryl destroyed everything she touched. When she was young, Penny had thought she'd been immune. That she was the one thing Cheryl had wanted to keep. Boy, had she been wrong. As she got older, Penny realized that she had just been in the way. More trouble than she'd been worth. Even though yesterday her mother had assured her that she loved her, how was that possible when she'd left her like discarded trash all those years ago?

"That's real mature of you, Penny." Bitsy glanced at her watch. "Oh, I have to run. Things to do, you know."

Most likely Bitsy wanted to go from store to store to tell everyone about their conversation. The bell rang as Bitsy went out the door, throwing a goodbye behind her as she went.

A year? Cheryl never committed to anything longer than month to month. How would she ever fit in in this small town? The nearest bar was over in Owen. Did she even have a car? A license? How did she have money to pay the security deposit on a house?

Cheryl had been pretty hard up for money when she'd dropped Penny off years ago. Hadn't she said she'd wound up in rehab because of being arrested? Or had Penny filled in that part herself?

The door rang again. Penny held her breath as she peeked around the corner. A couple, probably from out of town, walked in.

"If you need any help with anything, just holler," she said and turned back to the shelf she was reorganizing.

"Thanks," the man said.

When minutes went by and the door jingled again, she figured the couple had left. She didn't like to police her store by hovering over customers. It made people feel uncomfortable if she stood up front and stared at them while they browsed.

She went back to her register and looked over the monthly receipts.

"I love what you've done with the shop."

Penny froze, then lifted her gaze to her mother's. Her eyes darted to the back, where the couple was looking at furniture.

"Thanks." Penny didn't want her mother here. This was hers. Her safety net. Her roots. Everything her mother had never given her. It was Penny's and she didn't want her mother to destroy that. But she couldn't exactly throw a fit with customers in the back.

"I'm sorry I came over unannounced last night."

"You mean like you are doing now?"

Cheryl grinned sheepishly. "I had a feeling you wouldn't want to meet up for lunch or dinner after last night. If the only way to see you is to just pop up, then that's what I'm going to do."

"Gee, aren't I lucky?" Penny's voice might have been deadpan, but her heart was racing as if the devil himself was chasing her. The antiques store's high ceilings and large rooms seemed to close in around her. If she didn't get some air soon, she might pass out.

"Breathe, Penny," her mother said calmly.

Penny pulled in a breath and then another.

Her mother had the gall to look hurt. "I swear I didn't come back to upset you."

"You don't upset me. You don't do anything to me." She wasn't fooling Cheryl and she knew it.

"I promised to come back."

"Excuse me, but what is the price of this plate?" the woman said.

Penny pulled her gaze away from Cheryl and focused on the costumer. She put on her best smile and glanced at the plate. "That one is a 1938 Wedgwood nonhunting dog plate with poodles called March Winds. It runs around one hundred and fifty online, but I'd be willing to bargain if you are interested."

The woman glanced back at the man with a pleading look on her face.

The man shook his head but got out his wallet. "Would you take one-thirty for it?"

"For you two? Of course." Penny held out her hand for the plate.

The woman beamed. Cheryl slipped away from the counter as Penny conducted the sales transaction. Penny tried to ignore her mother's wanderings, but the back of her neck prickled.

"There you go. I added a care instruction sheet in there. Have a safe trip." Penny handed the bag to the woman, who hadn't stopped grinning.

The man put his hand on the woman's back and led her to the door as if he were afraid she might find something else.

"Thank you," he called out.

"Come again," Penny said. As soon as the door closed, the smile fell off her face.

She found Cheryl in the toy aisle. Penny kept her inventory low on these items because they weren't big sellers around here, but occasionally someone wanted something that they'd had as a child. Penny herself didn't have good memories associated with her childhood toys.

"You know, I don't think Mom would have thought of toys as antiques," Cheryl said as she picked up an old spinning top. "She always wanted this to be a classy store with only antiques from overseas."

"Classy stores don't do well in the country." Penny looked around to make sure Cheryl hadn't pocketed anything.

"She never understood that." She set down the top and faced Penny. "I know she wasn't the easiest person to live with, but she was good to you, wasn't she?"

Penny crossed her arms over her chest. "If you had cared, maybe you should have checked up on us. But then again, you just didn't care enough about me."

"I deserve that." Cheryl put her hands in her back pockets and looked down at the floor. "I wanted to come back, but I knew you were better off without me."

"How would you know?" Penny dropped her arms, walked behind the front counter and pretended to study a list of recent transactions. Her mother could run off with the whole inventory for all she cared, as long as she left.

Penny was done. This wasn't supposed to happen. Her mother had been long gone. She had no right to show up now. Penny didn't need her anymore.

"Mother wrote me."

Penny didn't look up from the figures, but they blurred before her eyes.

"She told me all about you and school and your friend Maggie." Cheryl sighed. "How could I come back and ask you to come live with me when you were clearly happier without me? How could I take care of you when I couldn't even take care of myself?"

"I could take care of myself."

"Exactly. What type of mother was I that my daughter took better care of me than I did of her? Everything you said last night was true. The men, the drinking. I couldn't control myself. I didn't want my addiction to hurt you any more than it already had." Cheryl brushed tears from her cheeks.

"Do you know how hard it was to call my mother, let alone drive back to this godforsaken town and give you to her?" Cheryl laughed bitterly. "I couldn't put you in the foster system. I was afraid I'd never get you back out of it. Plus I've heard about what happens to some kids in the system and you were already starting to develop…"

Penny pushed away from the counter. Her mother's "dates" had definitely begun to notice her development. She could still feel their hot gazes and subtle remarks.

Crossing her arms over her chest, Penny glared at Cheryl. "What do you want from me? Money?"

"No. No," she said firmly. "It took me a year of sobriety to get here because I wanted to be able to stay. I worked hard and saved every cent I made. I knew it wouldn't be easy coming back, but the only person's approval I need is yours."

Penny pressed her lips together tightly.

"I swear to you, I'm not out for anything except you. I know you don't believe it, but I love you, Penny. I've already applied for a waitressing job at The Rooster Café. I'm going to rent one of the houses in town. I'm staying—"

"Until you fall off the wagon."

"No, baby." Cheryl looked her in the eyes. "I'm staying for good."

Chapter Seventeen

"I promised you dinner and a movie." Luke held up a bag of groceries and a DVD.

"I hope you aren't looking for homemade from me because I'm no Betty Crocker." Penny stepped aside to let him in.

"I'll have you know that not only did I attend medical school, but I also learned to cook decent-tasting food on a small allowance every week." Luke started pulling out the ingredients. "Besides, if it really sucks, I've got a twenty in my wallet for pizza."

Penny smiled. "I suppose I can risk food poisoning as long as there's a backup plan."

He leaned in and kissed her. "That's my girl."

She flushed with warmth and sat at the kitchen table. This was just what she needed. No strings, no future commitment, just here and now with Luke. He wasn't pressing her to be family with him or to let him back into her life. No, it was just casual sex with the bonus of spending time together.

So what if she was head over heels in love with him? It wasn't as if that would make a difference, and it shouldn't. They could just keep having sex until he left for St. Louis.

She rubbed at the sudden ache in her chest. She needed a distraction from her crazy thoughts. "Okay, what are you going to make me?"

He wiggled his eyebrows mischievously. "Let's see if you can guess from the ingredients."

She raised her eyebrow in retaliation. "What part of 'I'm no Betty Crocker' did you not understand?"

"That's okay—I just want the saucy part of you."

"Good answer."

"I was a straight-A student."

"Mostly."

"Hey, everyone has an off year." He tweaked her nose for that one.

"I had twelve of them."

"I know for a fact you did much better your senior year." He sorted his groceries on her counter. "You can't tell me you didn't do well in kindergarten. I've seen you color. You *mostly* get it inside the lines."

Her mouth dropped open in mock indignity. "Mostly?"

"You've always been a little bit of a rebel." He winked at her.

She chuckled. "You've got me there."

He started opening and closing her drawers, pulling out a knife and then a cutting board. "I bet you would have done awesome if you'd had a fair shot at school."

Some of her lightheartedness fled at the reminder of her mother. "Probably not. Like you said, I was always a rebel."

"You know if you want to talk about it, I'm here." He glanced up at her as he cut a tomato.

"I didn't think you'd know that much about being a rebel." She touched her finger to her lip in mock surprise. "Oh, wait, you did have that one year.... How many fights did you get in? Five or six?"

"Seven." Luke set aside the diced tomato and started cutting a garlic clove. "All but two were off school property."

"And what did those boys do to deserve your anger?" She reached over and plucked a chunk of tomato off the cutting board and popped it in her mouth.

"Is it bad if I say I don't remember?" He glanced at her sheepishly, then sliced a green pepper.

She laughed. "I wouldn't believe you. That giant brain of yours won't let you forget anything."

It was what she'd counted on when she decided to kiss Sam. Luke would remember every time some guy had implied he'd banged her.

"Yeah, well," he said, "some things I wish I could forget and others I wish I remembered better."

"What do you wish you remembered?"

Luke rinsed his hands and pulled out a saucepan and a stockpot. "My childhood. My parents. Sam and Brady before our parents died. Every now and then I catch a memory, but they are few and far between. I can't remember much before I became angry all the time."

She watched him as he added his chopped ingredients to the saucepan and set a pot of water to boil. "And here I keep wishing I could forget my childhood, but that's not going to happen now that Cheryl is in town."

"Do you want wine or something else to drink?" He held up a bottle of red.

"It's definitely a wine night." When he raised his eyebrow, she added, "In moderation."

He poured them both a glass. When he brought her glass to her, he leaned down and kissed her. Sparks sizzled through her at the contact.

"I don't think I could ever forget you." Luke straightened and winked before turning back to the stove.

"I hope not," she said softly, more to herself than to him. She hoped she was as scorched into his memory as he was in hers. After the past week and a half with him she was fairly certain that he'd ruined her for casual sex. It didn't help that she'd already been losing interest in it before he arrived. She still wanted sex, just not from some random guy. Actually only one guy would do now....

"So have you guessed what I'm making you yet?" Luke glanced over his shoulder.

"Hamburgers?"

"I don't even have ground meat."

"That's probably a good thing."

"Guess again."

"Hmm...tomatoes, garlic, pepper and some stuff in a jar.... Haggis?"

Luke turned and gave her the stink eye. "Haggis?"

"You mean I guessed right?" She grinned.

"If I didn't have to make sure the food didn't burn, I'd show you what I think of your guesses." He stirred the sauce and then added pasta to the boiling water.

"I'm just surprised you don't have garlic bread. After all, everyone knows garlic bread goes well with haggis."

He very carefully laid down his spoon, then turned and headed for her.

She tried not to giggle, but a few laughs slipped out. "Spaghetti! Spaghetti!"

"Too late." He yanked her up to standing and kissed her soundly. Without breaking the kiss, he lifted her against him and walked her back toward the stove.

She squealed when he lifted her higher and set her on the counter next to the cooking food. Without a word, he walked back to the kitchen table and grabbed her wine. He handed her the glass before resuming his stirring.

She crossed her legs, glad that she'd worn shorts today. Luke's gaze dropped to her calves. Everything felt wonderful. It was so easy to forget that Cheryl was in town and that Luke was leaving. This moment could last forever for all she cared.

"Isn't using the jar sauce cheating?" She lifted the empty jar off the counter behind her.

"Rather than spend hours waiting for the sauce to get ready, I'd rather spend the extra time making love with you."

Tingles coursed through Penny at the words *making love.* It meant nothing. Loads of people used that term for sex. Just because she was in love with him didn't make him in love with her.

"I add a few things to make their sauce a little richer. You'll notice I used store-bought pasta, too. Think of all the time I saved not doing that from scratch." His eyes raked her body from head to toe and back again.

"You better watch it, or dinner will burn and we'll be stuck with pizza."

"Thirty minutes for delivery time…." He looked as if he was contemplating it.

She laughed. "Forget it. You promised me a home-cooked meal, so you're stuck now."

"Good thing this is quick to prepare. The pasta only needs a few more minutes."

When he returned to stirring, she took in a deep

breath and filled her senses with rich garlicky tomato sauce and just a hint of Luke.

"I hope you are a fast eater." Luke lifted the pot and took it to the sink, careful not to lose any noodles as he poured out the water.

"Why is that?"

He put the pot down and lifted her from the counter. The kiss he gave her was less teasing and more ravenous. It lit an answering hunger from deep inside her that had nothing to do with food. His lips tasted of the red wine they'd been sharing.

When he released her, she leaned against the counter to regain her balance. "Good answer."

He grinned. "I can't wait to ace the final."

She pulled out two plates. He loaded their plates with pasta, sauce and garlic bread—which he'd waited to unpack from the sack. She refilled their glasses and they sat at the kitchen table.

"To healthy appetites." Luke lifted his glass.

She flushed with warmth from the look in his blue eyes. "To healthy appetites."

They made it about halfway through their dinner before he moved in for a kiss. They rose from the table as one and worked their way down the hall and up the stairs to her bedroom, chucking clothes as they went.

Right beside her bedroom door, he pinned her to the wall and pressed his naked body against hers. Her breath caught in her throat as he kissed his way down her neck and along her shoulder. His hands held hers against the wall as he dipped his head to take her breast into his mouth. She was helpless against the rising tide of passion that engulfed her. When she thought she could take no more, he pushed her just a little further over the edge until she forgot where he ended and she began.

He pulled her through the doorway to her bedroom. They fell together on the bed, consuming each other with hands and mouths, finding the spots that made her moan and him gasp. When he finally lifted above her and slowly entered her, she felt as if the fire in her had always been and would never find release.

Luke made the flames burn hotter with every stroke, every touch of his hands. Finally she reached the highest point and turned to ashes, floating back down into her body. He came down with her.

With the gentlest touch, he brushed her hair away from her face. Still joined, he lightly touched his lips against hers. She'd never felt more fulfilled, more cherished. More loved.

"This isn't just about sex anymore, Penny." Luke lay beside her with his shoulder touching hers and her hand in his. She wanted this and it was terrifying.

She stared up at the ceiling, willing her body to return to normal. Fighting to hold back from proclaiming her love. She didn't say anything. She couldn't. The one person she'd never wanted to lie to… The one person she always wanted to tell everything… But she couldn't ruin his future.

"Even as teenagers, I felt it. That this could be so much more."

"This is all we'll have, though," Penny whispered because if she said it too loud it would break her heart.

"Why?" He leaned up on his elbow and looked down at her.

It was harder to hide this way, lying naked with him. It wasn't the lack of clothing, but being in her bedroom, having him make love to her, having him care for her. It was all too much.

"You can never trust me." The words barely made any sound, yet they rang loud through the room.

"Have you had sex with anyone else since I arrived?" His hand trailed over the side of her breast, down over the dip in her waist and over her hip.

"No, bu—"

"Have you wanted to have sex with someone else since I arrived?"

She stared up at the ceiling. Everything in her screamed at her to tell him the truth. To stop playing the game. She shook her head no.

"All I ever wanted was you." He leaned down and kissed her lips.

"You shouldn't." Penny shook her head.

"Why not?" Luke's voice was seductive. "You're intelligent. Independent. Beautiful."

She rolled away from him. "You shouldn't want me. There are better women out there for you. Ones who aren't so…broken."

"Let me fix you." He stroked his hand down her back.

"I can't." She wanted nothing more than to sink back into his arms, but she knew if she did, she'd never have the strength to let go. "You know the type of woman I am."

"What type is that?"

Steeling herself, she sat up and turned to face him. "The kind who kisses your brother."

She saw the light go out of his eyes. She kept her head up, but inside her world was crumbling. Her stomach knotted and her throat seized closed. He turned from her and sat on the edge of the bed. Her eyes burned.

"So *you* kissed him?" His tone was even, not betraying one ounce of feeling.

"Yeah." She'd been strong enough to do it before, and she could do it again. She could push Luke away one last time and make this one stick. And she could just tell the truth.

"Why?" He turned and lifted his gaze to hers. His question held no accusation in it, just curiosity.

In all her lonely nights, she'd wondered the same damned question. Had she just been a scared little girl? Or had there been more to it? But for him, she'd brazen it out. Be the stronger of the two of them because she knew that Luke deserved better than her. "Maybe I wanted to know if he kissed like you."

"Did he?"

No one kissed like Luke. But admitting that wouldn't help him to leave her.

"Maybe I wanted to kiss every guy in Tawnee Valley and just needed to add Sam to my list." It felt as if there was a freight train rattling down the tracks toward her and she couldn't step out of the way. "Maybe all the rumors were true. Maybe I was the town slut."

He looked away from her, and she felt the hole beginning to form in her heart. This is where he'd walk away. It didn't matter how many days he had left before he went back to St. Louis. This would be when he walked away from her again.

She should be glad. This is what she wanted. What he needed.

"Bull."

"Excuse me?" she said. Her slowing heart picked up its tempo.

"You heard me," he said as he stood. He came around the bed and stood in front of her. "Bull."

"What the hell is that supposed to mean?" She tried to recapture her breath, but when he was near, the air disappeared.

"That was years ago. If you wanted to be the town slut, you could have been. Instead you were with me. You never once looked at another guy while we were together. I knew it. I saw it. You were mine and always have been."

"You don't know that." God, she wanted him to believe that. But she couldn't let him. If he'd said this to her after she'd kissed Sam, she would have lost her resolve to push him away.

He lowered his head until his lips were barely brushing against hers. "Yes, I do. Just like I know that you are mine now."

She wanted to shake her head no and go down swinging. Instead she got lost in his eyes, picking out the flecks of dark and light blue. His mouth captured hers and she gave up. Only for tonight.

She'd start the fight over in the morning, make him see that she wasn't what he wanted. That they wouldn't have a happily ever after because she wasn't built that way.

He pressed her back down onto the bed and into the mattress. Tomorrow was definitely soon enough.

Chapter Eighteen

"Sam?" Luke came in through the screen door followed by the bang. "Sam!"

"What?" Sam came out of the bathroom, drying his hair with a towel. He looked as he always did in jeans and a black T-shirt with the faded Metallica logo. It was hard to believe he had surgery less than a week ago.

"What happened that night?" Luke came to a halt in front of Sam and searched his face for clues. It was time to learn the truth, and he knew Penny wouldn't be the one to tell him. She was afraid of something. Getting to the bottom of his graduation night seemed like his best shot at convincing her they belonged together.

"What night?" Sam threw the towel back into the bathroom. His dark wet hair stood haphazardly around his head. He slicked a hand over it and headed to the living room.

Luke followed in his wake. "The night of my graduation. I saw you kissing Penny."

Sam sighed as he sat in his recliner. "I'm surprised you didn't bring it up before."

"Why would I?"

"Because I saw you walking off when I pushed her away." Sam rubbed a hand down his face.

That answered one question. Sam knew he'd seen him. "What happened?"

"You want a blow-by-blow?" Sam lifted his eyebrow as if to say, *Are you sure?*

Luke took in a deep breath and sat on the couch. "It's been years, but I need to know."

Something about the way she reacted when her mother had come back into her life unexpectedly had reminded him of right before graduation. They'd been talking about the coming year and how he'd be at University of Illinois and she'd come with him. Or more to the point, *he'd* talked about it. Now that he thought about it, the more he'd talked about it, the quieter and more distant she'd become.

"I went into the house to get a beer." Sam reached over and grabbed his glass of water. "I was surprised to find Penny in the room when I closed the refrigerator. She glanced out the door and then kissed me."

Luke remembered that part way too well. "You kissed her back."

The tips of Sam's ears turned red. "I'd had a couple of drinks and it'd been a while…. I pushed her away as soon as I realized what was happening. She looked out the door and I followed her gaze to see you walking away. She seemed satisfied with whatever she wanted to happen, but then she just collapsed. Sank to the ground like a stone."

Luke leaned forward, concentrating on every detail.

"I grabbed her elbow to help her up. She'd gone pale and was shaking all over. She kept repeating, 'He can't know, he can't know.' I had no idea what her problem was. She was your girlfriend, after all."

Sam shook his head. "I told her you saw us and she just nodded like she was numb. I told her I'd talk to you, but she grabbed my hand and said no."

"What happened next?" Luke's mind was spinning around the details.

"She got up, said she was sorry and went out the door. I didn't see her again that night." Sam shrugged. "I couldn't find you, and you left before breakfast the next morning. That was the day Brady told me he was going to London and I lost it."

"That was a rough day." Luke remembered when he got home that afternoon. He'd still been upset at Sam and Penny, but Brady had pulled him aside. Luke said to Sam, "Brady told me to watch over you. He said you acted like you didn't need anyone, but you did."

"Leave it to Brady to make it sound like a Hallmark card." Sam shook his head and rubbed his chest.

"Do you need a pain pill?" Luke started to get up, but Sam waved him off.

"I don't need to be babied." Sam leaned his recliner back. "I just need to take it easy, like you've told me a hundred times."

Luke searched Sam's face for signs of pain or distress from his heart surgery. He'd have enough time to think about what he'd learned when he was outside working. "Why didn't you ever bring the kiss up?"

"I didn't want to deal with it. You'd broken up with Penny. Brady had left. It seemed better to just leave well enough alone."

Luke's brow furrowed. "But I barely spoke to you when I came home."

Sam closed his eyes and smiled. "But you came home."

"He's fine. I'm not sure why you still call me when I know you call him every night, too." Penny put the TV on mute and leaned back on the couch.

"Uncle Sam's not good on the phone," Amber said.

"Don't his grunts come through okay?" Penny glanced at her nails. She should paint them. It would give her something to do tonight. Who knew who would show up at her door this time? Her mother? Luke? The Easter Bunny?

"That's not funny. Uncle Sam doesn't just grunt."

"But he does grunt a lot." Penny smiled.

"Okay, he does." Amber called something out that was muffled. "Mom says we're coming home in a couple days, so I shouldn't have to call you every night...."

"You can still call if you want." Penny stared at the image of the Winchesters driving down a dark road.

"Penny says I can call if I want," Amber yelled. After a pause, Amber said, "Okay, I have to go, but Mom wants to talk to you."

"Bye, sweetie." Penny picked up the remote and pressed pause. Talking with Maggie would take more than half her attention.

Penny could almost picture her friend in a sundress in a fancy hotel room, waiting to go out with her new family. God, she missed her.

"How are things going?" Maggie said.

"Fine." Penny couldn't disguise the strain in her voice. "You're on your honeymoon. You should be having fun, not talking on the phone."

"I have a few minutes. Brady took Amber down to the pool. Now spill."

"There's nothing to tell." She was dealing with everything the best she could on her own. Maggie needed to focus on having a good time.

"Please. I know your 'fine' is never fine. Is it Luke? Sam?"

That was the issue with being best friends. They were always in each other's business. It was the best and only relationship Penny had kept.

"You asked for it." Penny looked up at the ceiling. "Cheryl is in town."

"Your mother came back! And all you said was fine. This is big. Huge. What did she say? What did you say? Is she still there? Did she leave again?"

Penny sighed. "She's here. Not here, here. But she's looking for a place to rent in Tawnee Valley. She wants us to try to get to know each other again." The last sentence left a bad taste in her mouth. No matter how many times she thought about it, her mother being here was bad. How long before she fell off the wagon? How long before she made Penny believe she was here for good and then leave?

"Is she sober?"

"Yeah, for a year apparently." Penny rubbed the bridge of her nose.

"Wow. So you guys are talking?"

"Not exactly." Penny winced because this had always been a sticking point with her and Maggie. Maggie had begged her to track down her mother. Life was short and you never knew how much time was left. But Penny didn't want to let her mother back into her life just to watch her walk away again.

"Seriously?" Maggie took a deep breath—probably

preparing for her lecture. "How many people do you have in your life?"

"Counting you and Amber?"

"Exactly—me and Amber. I know you had something with Luke and I know you still feel something for your mother. You can't keep doing this, Penny."

"Doing what?"

"Pushing everyone away. I love you. I have always been there and I'm not planning on going anywhere, but…"

"But?"

"I can't be your everything." Maggie sighed. "I wish I could be there every minute of the day, but I can't. You need more than me. You need someone who you love and who loves you and supports you in ways I can't."

Penny rolled her eyes. "That's the honeymoon and too much Disney talking."

"Weren't you the one who encouraged me to try with Brady?"

"Yeah, but that was different."

"How is that differ—"

"Because you deserve happiness. You deserve love and devotion and a great guy and a great family."

Maggie's voice was soft when she spoke after a heartbeat. "And you don't?"

"No. I don't. I deserve to grow old and die alone."

"You don't mean that."

"What else do you want me to say?"

"I want you to say that you'll try. That you'll give your mother a chance to explain. That you'll give Luke a chance to love you. Not the you who was eighteen and impulsive, but this woman you've become. What's the worst that could happen?"

Penny shook her head, pressed her lips together and

clutched at the lump in her stomach threatening to come up. If Maggie were here in front of her, she would have pulled Penny into her arms and talked her down. But she wasn't here.

"I can't," Penny pushed past her lips.

"You know I'd kick your ass if I were there, don't you?" Maggie's voice was hard, but she could hear the frustrated love behind the hardness. "You are not less deserving than I am, Penny. You deserve love. You deserve happiness. You deserve to live a full life."

Penny swallowed.

"If *you* don't think you're worth it, remember that *I* believe you are. Just promise me you'll try."

Maggie's faith in her left Penny shaken.

"I'll try."

"Now, about Luke…"

Penny could hear the smile in Maggie's voice. "We don't have enough time to talk about Luke. You need to get back to your husband and daughter."

"You're no fun." Maggie's pout came through loud and clear over the telephone.

"Well, I could tell you about the sex toys—"

"Okay, you win. I love you, Penny."

"I love you, too."

Maggie hung up the phone, leaving Penny with a lot to think about. Her mother showing up in her life upset everything. She'd broken her rule about letting guys into her bedroom for Luke. She could sit and think all night or…she could continue to watch *Supernatural*.

Hmm…life decisions or the Winchester brothers. No contest.

She punched the play button. Just when she was getting into it and Sam and Dean, the main characters, were about to face the demon, the doorbell rang. It was only six and she wasn't expecting anyone. She stopped her DVR and went to the door.

"This better be good. You're interrupting Sam and—" Pulling open the door, she met Luke's shocked face. "Hey."

"Since I just left my brother at the farm, I'm assuming you mean another Sam?" Luke came in and she shut the door behind him.

"Why would I talk about your Sam?" Taking a deep breath in, Penny turned and faced him. "Why do you care what Sam I'm talking about?"

The phone rang before Luke could say anything. She held up a finger and walked back into her living room to pick up the phone. The number was unknown, but she'd rather deal with whoever was on the other end than talk with Luke about "where they were going."

"Hello?"

"Penny?" Cheryl's voice hit her hard. It would take a while for the shock of her mother's appearance to become part of her normal. Of course, that could change at any time. Her mother was prone to leaving.

Maggie told her to try. Penny straightened. "Yeah."

"I was wondering if you'd like to get lunch tomorrow. I just signed my lease on my house and wanted to celebrate with you."

As much as her head screamed, *It's a trap to lull you into believing she'll stay,* Penny ignored it. "Sure, lunch sounds good."

Luke moved into the room behind her and her heart ratcheted up a beat.

"Oh, that's great. I can't wait. I'll come by the store at noon."

"See you then." Penny cut off the call and set the

phone down. She put her hand over her racing heart. Her hands shook and the world shifted beneath her feet.

Luke's arms went around her from behind. "Are you okay?"

She leaned back into his warmth and tried to breathe normally, but the world wouldn't stand still even with Luke holding her.

"Let's sit down." Luke helped her to sit on the couch and then released her. He pressed Play on the TV and left the room.

As the Winchesters began their fight, Penny started to relax. Her heart managed to find a normal pace again. Nothing in the room spun. She took in a breath and then another.

Luke came in and handed her a glass of water before joining her on the couch.

"Thank you," she murmured.

"No problem." He didn't take his eyes off the screen. "Sam and Dean, huh?"

She flushed. "Yeah."

"Mind if I change the channel?" Luke picked up the remote.

"Afraid of a little competition?" She relaxed into his side. Her mother and Luke were just too much to take at the same time. She was glad he was here.

"I'm here. They aren't. No competition there." Luke stopped the recording and flipped to a movie.

If he didn't want to bring up the what's-happening-with-us talk, she was more than willing to let it go. She'd made a few strides forward with one relationship today. She didn't need to fix this thing with Luke at the same time.

She settled into the crook of his arm and stared blankly at the television. Tomorrow would be soon enough to talk.

Chapter Nineteen

Penny sorted her silverware and placed the napkin in her lap. Cheryl sat across from her, looking at her expectantly. At least Cheryl hadn't tried to hug her when she'd stopped by the shop to get her for lunch at the diner. Penny was fairly certain a panic attack would have devoured her whole if Cheryl tried to touch her.

"I don't know where to start." Cheryl laughed nervously.

Penny smiled tightly but didn't offer any suggestions. She'd promised Maggie she'd try, but she didn't have to like it.

"I know you work at the shop, but did you do anything before that? Did you go to college? How was high school? Did you have any serious boyfriends? Who was the guy who came over that night?"

"Whoa." Penny held up her hands. "One question

at a time and I have the right to refuse to answer any or all of them."

Cheryl nodded. But before she could ask anything, their waitress, Rachel Thompson, came over to take their order. When she left, Cheryl folded her hands on the table.

"Okay, let's start with something easy. Did you go to college?"

"No," Penny said and looked out the window, wishing she could be anywhere else but here.

"Why not? You were always such a smart girl." Cheryl's brow furrowed.

"I didn't have the best grades going into high school and apparently all that crap they taught us in elementary school really was the basis for everything we learned later. You don't get into college taking remedial courses." Penny stopped herself from adding that her mother was why she hadn't done well in elementary school. If Cheryl didn't know that, then they were going to have more than a rocky start.

"What about the community college?"

"Grandma needed help at the store." Penny shrugged. To be honest, every time she'd thought about taking classes, she'd thought of Luke. He'd been the best tutor she could have had, and taking classes would have only reopened that wound.

"I can't change the past, Penny." Cheryl looked down at her hands and had the decency to look remorseful. "If I could have controlled the addiction, I would have. It took me a long time to realize that the addiction was in control of me and not the other way around."

"Do you still want to drink?"

"Every day," Cheryl admitted. "It's easier now than

when I first went to rehab, but little setbacks in life have a way of triggering the desire to drink."

"At any moment you could disappear or, worse, stay around and be drunk off your ass all the time?" Penny didn't hide her bitterness.

"No. That's why I go to group and have a sponsor. Someone who can talk me down when I think I need a drink." Cheryl reached her hand out, but Penny pulled hers into her lap before Cheryl could touch her. Cheryl clasped her hands back together. "I swear I'm here to stay and I know you won't believe it until you see it, but I promise you—"

"Just like you promised to come back." Penny's head was starting to hurt. It didn't take much for the pain to resurface from all those years ago. "I waited for you. I didn't even unpack my bag for a year. I was always ready for when you'd come back and get me and we'd be a family again."

"I'm sorry—"

"That's not enough." Penny glanced around the diner and lowered her voice. "Sorry isn't worth anything. You not being there meant everything was wrong. Grandma kept telling me that I'd seen the last of you and I kept telling her she'd see in the morning. You would be here then and I'd be gone. Do you know what that does to someone? To constantly be waiting for someone who never comes back?"

"No, I don't know what it was like for you." Cheryl didn't move.

"It hurts. I cried every day. I didn't make friends because I wouldn't be here long enough. Maggie was the only one who understood me. I didn't build a relationship with my grandma. I kept everyone away because I would leave as soon as you came back for me."

Cheryl pressed her lips together, but her eyes looked as if she wanted to say she was sorry.

"Do you know how hard it is to let someone in when you've kept everyone away for so long?"

"Yes, I do." Cheryl's words stopped Penny cold.

"What?"

"I know what it's like to shut down and not trust anyone. I trusted your father. He'd been my first love. Sure, my mom called me wild in high school, but I'd only been with him. When I got pregnant and Mom kicked me out, I went to him."

Penny leaned forward. Her mother had never talked about her father before. She hadn't even been aware that he'd lived in Tawnee Valley.

"We were so stupid. Or at least I was. He came with me to start a new life. We didn't get married right away, but we talked about it. We didn't have much money and I'd already started showing. We needed to save up for you, so we put it off. I was working one night and got sick, so I came home early and found him with someone else."

Cheryl stopped and took a drink of her Diet Coke. Her eyes were glazed from remembering the past.

"I tore into him. He had become my world. The only person I could trust, and he was sleeping with anyone who made eyes at him. I blew up and told him to leave and never come back."

Penny swallowed the lump that had formed. She'd never thought her father might have been bad for them. She thought he'd left because of her.

"I wasn't thinking. All these feelings had been going through me. How could he do that to me? To us? I didn't think he'd stay away. We'd had fights before, but this was different. I wasn't even sure I would have taken him back if he'd showed up." Cheryl's eyes were filled with regrets.

"Did he ever contact you?" Penny couldn't help the hope in her voice. Her father hadn't left because of her. He'd left because he was two-timing her mother. Yet he hadn't come back to be with his daughter. But it hadn't just been her.

"No. After you were born, I was sure he'd come back, but he didn't. At some point I realized he wasn't coming back and tried to date, but the only thing that made me feel like dating was the numbness of alcohol. I knew it was bad and that I was letting you down, and that made me feel worse so I'd drink more."

"You tried...." Try as she might, Penny couldn't forget the good times with her mother. When she'd get a job and drink only in the evenings. Things always seemed better then.

"I did, but it never stuck. I'd meet a guy and start thinking he'd cheat on me or leave me or both and I'd drink." Tears filled her eyes. "I wanted so badly to stop for you. But I couldn't go to rehab and take you with me. I was lucky that Child Protective Services didn't step in earlier."

Cheryl reached across the table. "I left you so that I could get help to deserve you."

Penny stared at Cheryl's open, grasping hand. How easy would it be to just accept what she was offering? Put her hand in hers and have a mom again? How much heartbreak could she stand if she opened herself up to Cheryl and she left again?

She clasped her hands to keep from reaching out and shook her head to remind herself that this wasn't real.

Rachel stopped by with their food. Penny stared down at the burger and fries. She'd been hungry before, but now with all this new information swimming in her brain, she felt too overloaded.

"Aren't you going to eat?" Cheryl asked.

"Yeah." Penny shook herself out of it. "Of course."

She took a big bite of the burger and chewed. It tasted like sawdust in her mouth.

"Did you go to your prom?"

Penny blushed and finished swallowing the burger. That night she and Luke had had every intention of attending prom, but one thing had led to another... Technically they had gone to their prom. They just never made it into the gym, where the dance was being held. "Yes."

"Was there someone special?" Cheryl looked more relaxed now that they were talking about little stuff.

Penny wished she could relax, too, but Luke was a sticking point for her. She'd loved him forever and thinking back to high school... It all had been simple until graduation.

"Yeah, I had someone." She wiped her mouth with the napkin and flagged down Rachel. "Can we get the check?"

"Sure thing."

Penny placed the napkin on the table. "I really need to get back to the shop."

Her mother set down her fork. "Of course. I wouldn't want to keep you from your business. It seems important to you."

"It is." It was the only constant in her life. Even now when everything else was spiraling out of control, the shop was still there. All her antiques were on their shelves, exactly where they belonged. And when she was in there, she could try to forget about Luke and Cheryl. It didn't always work, but she could try.

"I'm glad you have something." Cheryl smiled. "Could we try to get together again this week?"

The world hadn't opened up and swallowed her whole from this lunch. Maybe she could rebuild a relationship with her mother. Or maybe she'd be better off cutting her losses now and telling Cheryl to find someone else to make amends to. "I'll check my schedule."

Luke checked his watch. It was only nine o'clock, but all the lights were off at Penny's house. He knew he should just go home. Sam was doing fine. Instead he parked his car and walked up to the front door.

He pressed the doorbell and Flicker barked from somewhere in the house. A light flicked on in the hallway and Penny emerged in her light blue cotton pajamas. He drank in the sight of her as she made her way to the door. Her ginger hair was tousled as if he'd woken her.

A moment of worry went through him. What if she was sick? What if she was with someone else?

She opened the door after checking to make sure it was him. "Hey."

"Are you okay? Are you sick?" Luke pressed his hand to her forehead.

She scowled at him and swatted his hand away. "I'm fine. I don't need you to play doctor."

"But that's my best role." He winked.

She just rolled her eyes. "Come on in. You can watch me sleep if you want."

"I didn't mean to wake you." Luke closed and locked the door behind them. "Usually you don't go to bed until later."

"*Usually,* I don't have a man keeping me up all hours

of the night." She raised an eyebrow and quirked the side of her mouth up in a little smile.

"I can go…." He put his thumb out to point to the door.

She smiled. "Don't be silly. You're better than an electric blanket and the dog combined."

She grabbed the waistband of his jeans and pulled him down the hallway to her bedroom. "Beat it, Flicker. I've got someone who won't hog the covers."

Flicker whined and looked at her from the bed with the most pathetic look Luke had ever seen a dog give.

"You had your chance, cover hog. Get!" Penny pointed to the door and the dog huffed his way off the bed and out of the bedroom. She closed the door behind him. "Now, where were we?"

"You were comparing me to heating devices?" Luke leaned against the wall next to her dresser.

"Ah, yes. You are definitely my favorite toy. And to think you don't even need batteries, and you're waterproof." Her pajama shorts revealed her long legs and hung low on her hips. Her top barely covered her breasts.

His body twitched in reaction. "I'd like to think I'm more than just a walking heated toy."

She advanced on him like a predator. "Mmm…you are so much better than any toy I've owned."

She stopped a hair's breadth away from him. As he inhaled her sweet scent, her breasts touched his chest. Something was off, though, and it wasn't just that she'd been sleeping.

"Maybe we should check to see if you need fresh batteries." She grinned as she cupped him.

He hardened against her hand. It had never taken much for Penny to get him going, but the past few days, she'd been different. More open. More emotional. Now it seemed as if she'd bottled that back up and was using the sexpot angle again. He shouldn't mind. They had only a few days left together.

Maggie and Brady would be home the day after tomorrow, and he'd need to get back to St. Louis. And this thing between them would end. But should it? Instead of stumbling through life numb, he could have Penny to come home to. It had been almost a decade since high school, and even though they'd changed, the chemistry between them hadn't.

They were combustible when mixed. He didn't want to leave her, but would she be willing to come with him? One thing had to be cleared up first.

Penny pressed her body against his and pulled his head down to meet her lips. His arms went around her and lifted her against him for the perfect fit. Her mouth tasted of vanilla ice cream and he couldn't get enough.

Before he was completely gone, he lifted his head. "We need to talk."

"Ugh. I've talked already today." She wove her fingers through his hair and tugged his head down. "I just want to play with my toy."

She nipped at his bottom lip. As enticing as the offer was, he needed to sort this out. Their time together was closing fast.

"I'll make you a deal." He shifted his hands to more comfortably hold her against him.

"I'm listening." She stared at his lips as if waiting for the right moment to pounce.

He gritted his teeth as she moved against him. The importance of talking was slowly ebbing; his body had other things it needed at the moment. "Maybe we can do both."

"Talk and sex? How original." She rolled her eyes.

"Next you'll be showing me a new sandwich made with peanut butter *and* jelly."

Instead of answering, he kissed her. She murmured something against his lips, but then softened against him. He walked them back until they hit the bed and lowered them both to the mattress.

"Is this really what you sleep in?" He lifted his head and gazed down at her exposed stomach. He ran his palm across it and watched her quake in response. "No wonder you are cold."

"I suppose you have flannel pajamas instead." Penny pulled his T-shirt out of his jeans and inched it upward. "Mmm. Maybe you wear nothing at all."

He helped her get his shirt off, but when she reached for his pants, he stalled her hand. "Not yet."

She pouted and pressed her hand against his abs, making him tighten them in response. "I guess this is the talking part?"

"The kiss with Sam—"

"Again?" Penny flopped back against the bed and put her arm over her eyes. Her shirt rose, revealing the underside of her breast.

"I just want to understand what made you run before." He managed to keep his hand on her stomach.

"What makes you think I was running?" She lifted her arm slightly to meet his eyes.

"You went to Sam and kissed him. You knew I would see you."

She put her arm back over her eyes. "Maybe I was drunk. Why are we obsessing over something that happened almost ten years ago?"

"Because it changed us." He pried her arm off her eyes and held her hand. "I thought we were on the same page. That you were coming with me to college. That eventually we'd get married and start a family."

"Do I look like a fairy tale to you?" She raised her eyebrow.

"It doesn't have to be a fairy tale, if it's true." Luke rested his elbow on the bed and leaned his head on his hand. "Hindsight is twenty-twenty. I didn't realize then that I'd been the one doing all the planning. We were following my dream because I thought it was our dream. But the more I talked, the more you acted like this."

She pressed her lips together.

"You can't deny that you shut down your emotions." Luke ran his hand across her stomach to keep from exploring the soft skin under her shirt. "You bottle them up so tight that you practically implode. Like last night."

"I don't want to play this game anymore."

"It's not a game, Penny. It never was." Luke used his knuckle to turn her face so she'd look at him. "I love you. I always have. You're the reason I couldn't move on. Even after seeing you kiss Sam, I wanted you in my life, but it drove me crazy thinking of you with other guys."

"But that's who I am. It's who I was and it's who I became." She wouldn't look him in the eyes.

Every part of him knew she was lying. "I'd believe that if you hadn't collapsed after kissing Sam. I'd believe that if I didn't know that you never looked at anyone else but me when we were dating. I'd believe that if you were a better liar."

"You believed it then. You believed it all. That I kissed Sam because I wanted to. That everything everyone had said about me was true."

"I was stupid and afraid." Luke didn't stop looking in her eyes. "It was easier to think the worst of you than to admit that I loved you but you didn't want to be with me."

"I wanted to be with you. I've always wanted you."

"Then what happened?"

She looked away from him.

"Don't hide from me. Don't lie. I have to go in a couple days and I don't want to leave this unfinished with me always wondering and you going on the way you did after I left."

"What if the truth hurts too much?"

"Then we'll face it together."

"What if it doesn't change anything?"

"It doesn't have to. It won't change the way I feel about you." He kissed her briefly, and when she opened her eyes, he said, "I love you."

She shook her head, rejecting his declaration, but it didn't matter. It wouldn't change the way he felt about her. Or the fact that he wanted her in his life, but he knew they had to overcome the past to start building a future. He also knew that he had to go slowly with her. Something was holding her back even now.

"It doesn't matter how much you love me…you'll leave me." Her voice was even. She believed every word that passed her lips. "Everyone who loves me leaves me. My dad, my mom, you."

"I wouldn't have left you—"

"Yes, you would have." She propped herself up on her elbows. "We would have gone off to follow your dream and you would have decided I was not smart enough or not pretty enough or you just would have been done with me. And I would have been left alone in a strange town with no family and no friends."

"I wouldn't have—"

"Wouldn't you have?" Penny pushed up to sitting and

grabbed a pillow to hold in front of her. A tear trailed down her cheek. "How long did it take you to believe the worst in me after seeing me kiss Sam?"

His heart thundered in his chest. She was right. He'd made the connections quickly because she'd been distant.

"Exactly. You didn't even come to me and ask me to clear it up. You just left. You didn't even say goodbye."

"What can I say, Penny? I thought I'd lost you. I was terrified of ending up hurt and in that dark place I'd been in after my parents died." He didn't ever want to experience that again. The rage, the pain, the bleakness.

"But you didn't." Her smile was sad. "Because life without me was so much better than life with me. Admit it. You did better in school because I wasn't there to weigh you down."

"You never weighed me down. You lifted me up out of a bad situation. You always have. That night in the hospital, when you so easily could have gone home and not given me another thought, you stayed. You took my mind off what was happening with Sam. When I'm with you, I feel alive. I don't know how to explain it better."

He grabbed her hands and pressed them to his heart. "If I have to, I can *survive* without you in my life, but I can't *live* without you. I love you."

"It won't work," she said softly. "We are too different now. We both have our own lives. I have the shop and you work at a hospital. We have lives that don't intersect except for this one time. Can we just enjoy the time we have left?"

He wanted to press her. To insist that they could be more. That together they could solve any problem. But the harder he pushed her, the more closed off she'd get. He could see that now.

"Yeah, we can enjoy what time we have left, but I want you to know, I would never willingly leave you."

Chapter Twenty

Penny threw down the stack of papers she was organizing and stared out her shop window. Luke loved her. How was she supposed to process that information?

If it were any other guy, she'd have laughed at him or kicked him out of her bedroom last night. But with Luke, she'd curled up in his arms and slept. Well, she slept after he'd made love to her.

Maggie and Brady came back tomorrow. Sam was feeling better every day. Between Brady and Jasper, the farmwork would be taken care of, so Luke could go back to his big-city living and find that girl who was going to keep his house and give him two point five children.

That wasn't going to be her. The sharp pain in her chest wanted to say differently, but she wasn't going to listen to it. After everything her heart had been through, Luke wouldn't be the hardest thing to let go.

She'd done it once already. Next time should be a cakewalk because, although he said he loved her, she hadn't said it back. Admitting it out loud would have been her downfall. It was bad enough that she felt it.

The bell jingled above her door, bringing her back to today. She glanced at the middle-aged woman who came in.

"Let me know if I can help you find anything." Penny picked up her papers and tried to focus on the words again. In the past two weeks or so, she'd lost her focus. First Luke coming back, which would have been fine if it'd been confined to the wedding. But he'd been here longer and every time he came to her, she couldn't help but let him in.

Worse, she'd broken the rule of letting him into her bedroom. Now anywhere she went in her house, his ghost would haunt her long after he returned to St. Louis. Him leaning against the kitchen counter with his smile and telling her about the piglets on the farm. Him sitting next to her on the couch, quietly watching a movie together. Him sleeping next to her in her bed.

She sighed and set the papers down. There had to be something else she could work on.

The bell jingled. Her mother came in, glanced around and then focused on Penny.

"I swear I wasn't planning to stop by, but I got some terrific news." Cheryl set her purse down on top of the papers. Her hair was caught back in a ponytail and she wore the uniform of the waitstaff at The Rooster Café.

"Did you want me to guess?" Penny asked after a moment. She wasn't really interested, but apparently Cheryl had the best news in the world from the smile on her face.

"No, of course not. I mean how could you guess? I

know it's not the best timing, but when is it ever. I met someone."

Penny flinched as if Cheryl had slapped her across the face. She sank into the chair behind the register and waited for her heart to start beating again. This was how it always began. Cheryl was happy with a job and a place to live and then she met someone. It wouldn't be long before she started drinking again. And that's when things got rough.

"I just needed to share with someone." Cheryl hadn't noticed Penny's reaction yet. "I wanted to share with you. You are the reason I'm here, but...to have this opportunity, when I thought I was done with men."

That's when Cheryl turned around and noticed Penny. Penny couldn't breathe, let alone speak.

"Is something wrong?" Cheryl rushed around the counter and squatted next to Penny's chair. She reached out hesitantly, as if she was going to touch Penny's hand, but decided against it. "Are you okay?"

From the pit of Penny's stomach the old pain and longing rose to the surface. She looked Cheryl in the eyes. "You left me."

"I—"

"You left me alone and didn't come back. The one person in the world I had. The one person I loved. I trusted you and you left me all alone."

"It broke my heart to leave you. I did my best. I found you a home and somewhere you would be safe. I thought if I got help I could come back to you."

"But you didn't come back."

"No," Cheryl said slowly. "So many times I tried to get clean. I wanted to. I knew it was the only way to get you back. Mother made me promise. She made me—"

Cheryl covered her mouth as tears flowed down her

cheeks. "I had to prove to her that I was worthy of you. That was the only way she'd take you in. I told her about the men, the alcohol, selling your stuff. She knew that if she didn't take you in, I couldn't protect you. It was bad enough that I was with those type of men, but if they'd hurt you, I would have never forgiven myself."

Penny couldn't respond. What was there to say that hadn't already been said?

"Every time I thought I was getting close, something would happen. I was afraid I'd never make it back to you. So I drank."

"What's different about this time? Tell me so I can believe you. Make me understand why you are waltzing back into my life seventeen years later and expecting to have some sort of relationship with me, when all I can think about is when you are going to leave me again." Penny kept her voice down; inside she felt cold and hollow.

"Don't say that, Penny-pie. Please don't say that. I'm never going to leave again. I'm never going to drink again. If it means that I grow old alone but get to be with the one thing that I did that was ever worthwhile, I can do it. I can do it for you." Cheryl brushed a strand of hair out of Penny's eyes.

"Don't do it for me." Penny grabbed Cheryl's hands and held them still. "Don't do it for me. Do it for you because you want to. Because you need to. Because I won't be held responsible for the next time you fall down that rabbit hole. I won't be responsible when you pick up a drink because you've had a bad day or week or your boyfriend isn't treating you right. I won't be responsible for you."

Cheryl straightened. "You're right. It's my fault you took on so much when you were growing up. You don't need to be responsible for me anymore. I will stay clean for me and for you, but if I do stumble, please don't shut me out. I'm not perfect. I make mistakes."

Penny felt the beginnings of a smile. "I'm not going anywhere."

"Neither am I. And if you think I shouldn't date—"

"Please, I'm hardly the authority on dating." Penny laughed and stood. "Just don't let it get bad. Make sure to end it before it gets bad."

"Promise." Cheryl walked around to the other side of the counter and leaned across it. "So let me tell you about Paul."

Penny opened the screen door of the farmhouse as the car stopped in the driveway. The two farm dogs crowded around the car and barked. Luke was already coming down from the field. Sam was inside snoring on the recliner. She wouldn't be surprised if the dogs woke him up with their insistence that the household needed to be alerted to the arrival of outsiders.

The car doors opened, and Amber was the first to be greeted by the dogs. Maggie and Brady got out while they were distracted. Penny's chest felt lighter seeing her best friend. Penny and Maggie hugged as soon as they were close enough. They hadn't been apart much in the years since high school.

"You look wonderful," Penny said. Maggie wore a sundress with a white shrug over it. She looked more than wonderful; she looked relaxed and happy.

"You haven't been eating, have you?" Maggie put her hand on Penny's cheek.

"I've been eating fine, Maggie."

"How's Sam been?" Brady asked before hugging Penny, too.

"Besides bored out of his mind, he's been fine."
Penny led them inside. Her pot of potatoes had started
to boil, so she turned down the stove a little to keep it
from boiling over.

"I'll go find Sam." Brady left the kitchen.

"So what's new?" Maggie sat at the kitchen table
and grabbed a handful of M&M's from the candy dish.

"In this kitchen, not much." Penny used stirring to
keep from meeting Maggie's gaze.

"You're lucky that I missed you and your quirky
ways." Maggie popped an M&M in her mouth. "Tell
me about your mother."

"Cheryl's fine. She's got a job, a house and a potential love interest."

"What about your relationship with her?"

"We're working on it. It won't fix itself overnight."
Penny stirred the potatoes and set the lid over them.

Maggie hugged her from behind. "I'm glad you are
trying."

"Me, too." She patted Maggie's arm.

Maggie sank back into her chair and Penny joined
her at the table. The screen door opened, and Amber
and Luke came in. Amber was talking his ear off about
some ride at Disney. Luke glanced Penny's way.

She couldn't keep her smile down, but she dropped
her gaze. She loved him, and just seeing him made her
feel warm and gooey inside. But the time to deal with
Luke was coming. She wanted to avoid it so she focused
on living in this moment. This could end only one way.

Amber ran up and tackle-hugged Penny. "I missed
you, Penny."

"I missed you, too, munchkin."

"Where's Uncle Sam?"

"I think he's in the living room with your dad." Luke

pointed in that direction and she was off. He stood there undecided for a moment.

"You can join us if you like. We're just catching up," Maggie said.

"I'd hate to be a third wheel. I'll go see what my brothers are talking about. I have to give Brady the grand tour of everything that is happening on the farm anyway and try to get Sam to sit it out."

"Good luck," Penny said.

He nodded and rubbed the back of his neck as he headed out of the room.

"So…" Maggie pointedly glanced at the door that Luke had disappeared through.

"So what?" Penny grabbed an M&M. How could she begin to talk about Luke when she didn't know what was going on herself?

"Penny?" Maggie put her hand over hers on the table. "Oh, sweetie, you've fallen for him again, haven't you?"

That's the thing that sucked about a best friend. They could see through any of the bull you put up for everyone else.

"Have you guys talked about the future?" Maggie asked with her concerned face on.

"What's there to talk about? I can't just leave What Goes Around Comes Around. I'm only just making a name for it. He's not going to give up his job at the hospital in St. Louis to come here…for what? To work in the hospital in Owen or drive all the way to Springfield for work every day."

"But you've thought about it."

"Of course I've thought about it. It's the only thing I can think about. That or my mother, and neither of them are very conducive to sleeping, eating or working."

Maggie squeezed her hand. "I bet if we put our heads together we could figure out something."

"It won't matter. What we have won't last."

"Why not?" Their heads both turned to see Luke standing in the doorway. "Why won't we last, Penny?"

Penny swallowed hard.

"Oh, I think someone is calling me." Maggie started to get up, but Penny gripped her hand tighter and gave her the please-don't-leave-me look. Maggie yanked her hand away and mouthed, "You'll be fine."

She hoped Maggie could read faces because hers was screaming, *Traitor!*

Maggie patted Luke's shoulder as she passed him. And to think Penny actually encouraged Maggie to go after Brady.

Luke took Maggie's seat at the table and continued to look at Penny, waiting for her explanation.

She opened her mouth and closed it. "We… I mean… There's just no… Can't we talk about this later?"

"When, Penny?" Luke leaned back in the chair and folded his hands behind his head. "Later today, tonight, tomorrow, or is later when I'm gone and you don't have to deal with what's going on between us?"

Heat rushed to her face. "We're just having fun while you are here."

The words sounded false to even her ears. Maybe if she hadn't said them like a question…

Luke nodded solemnly. "Sure."

The word cut into her heart. Even though she knew that's what they'd been doing, it had seemed more real than that to her. Maybe it had meant more to her than to him. It didn't matter. It had to end, and if she wanted to save her sanity, maybe now was the time to end it.

"After all—" she got up and checked on the pots on

the stove "—we were just teenage sweethearts. It's not like we could have ever made it work. Our relationship was built on rampaging hormones."

"Is that what you really believe?" Luke didn't move and his inflection didn't change to show any emotions.

"Every night we spend together is just about chemistry." She tried to make it sound believable.

"It wasn't just about sex." Luke stood up and looked out the window above the sink.

"So we had a few laughs. I cried on your shoulder. That's what friends do, right?" She walked across the room to stand as far away from him as possible when she faced him. "We're just friends."

"If you believed that, you wouldn't need to put so much distance between us. And I'm not talking about physical distance."

"I do believe it. What do you want from me?"

"In truth?"

"Yes, please tell me. I'm dying to know." She crossed her arms over her chest.

"The truth is I want you, Penny." He turned and slowly closed the distance between them. "I want you when you are laughing at a game of cards. I want you when you are mad at me for something little I did. I want you when you go sexpot on me to hide how you really feel. I want you when you cry in my arms."

He stopped in front of her and put his hands on her arms. "I want you with me. Morning, noon and night. I love you and nothing is going to change that."

Her insides felt heavy. She wanted to throw herself into his arms and say yes, but what if it all went wrong? "I can't. My shop, my house, my life…it's here."

"And no one can take those away from you."

She shook her head and pulled away. "I can't just leave. Maggie—"

"Has Brady now. You won't be gone forever."

"No." Tears flowed down her face. "No. I can't. I can't."

She stumbled to the door and jerked it open. The warm air hit her in the chest and stopped her breathing. *Turn around. Go back.*

She couldn't. She stood in the driveway with no purse and no keys. She'd have to go back in to get them, but that meant facing Luke. If he hadn't already followed her out....

The screen door screeched on its hinge and banged shut like a gun. She didn't turn. She didn't want to know. Luke had just handed her his heart on a platter and she'd shoved it back at him. How could she claim she loved him when she couldn't even accept his words?

"Hey," Maggie said.

Penny spun around and swiped at the tears on her cheeks. "Hey."

"I thought you might want these." She held out Penny's purse and keys.

"Thank you." Penny stepped closer to claim them, but Maggie held them back.

"Think about it." Maggie gave her her things. "Just think about what you really want and need. I know you're scared. I was scared, too, but this isn't just kids playing at being in love. I know Luke loves you. I've seen it in his eyes when he looks at you. And I know you love him, too."

Penny shook her head.

"Don't deny it. You might be able to hide from everyone else, but you can't hide from me." Maggie wrapped her arms around Penny.

She leaned into the hug, wishing she knew what to do.

"Whatever you decide," Maggie said, "I'll support you. You aren't alone."

Chapter Twenty-One

Luke sat on the couch and watched a show he hadn't caught the name of with Sam.

"Aren't you going out?" Sam asked.

"Not tonight." He'd considered going over to Penny's, but with the way things ended only a few hours ago, he thought it was best to let her have her space. For now.

"Penny's a good person." Sam leaned farther back in his recliner.

"I know that." Luke picked up his beer and took a swig from it.

"She's actually really responsible. I never picked up on that when you two were going out."

"I know that, too."

"She's brought in people from all over to visit her shop."

"Dammit, Sam, what's your point?"

"I can see why you like her, is all."

"Really? Wow, thanks. I was just about to ask your permission to court her." Luke rolled his eyes and stared at the cops trying to solve a case.

"No need to bite my head off. If you want to leave, I won't stop you."

"I think I'll stay right here."

"What, so she can get it in her mind that you really don't care that much about her? Can you blame the girl for being a little leery of you? After all, she kissed me once and you assumed she'd banged the entire student population. Trust is a two-way street."

"Big words from the guy who for eight years with-held the fact that Brady knocked up Maggie."

Sam held his hands up. "I have my own devils to deal with."

"Penny's just not ready." Luke shook his head.

"Will she ever be?"

"I hope so."

He was leaving tomorrow. Maggie had told her at the shop that afternoon. For the rest of the afternoon, Penny had been out of it. She caught herself staring at the door as if waiting for someone to come in.

Home alone that evening, she couldn't get settled. Not even watching *Supernatural* appealed to her. When she started to pace, Flicker barked at her.

"Screw it." She went to the bedroom and changed from her pajamas into a pair of cutoffs and a pink tank top. She let Flicker out one last time before grabbing her keys.

The drive out to the farm took ten minutes flat. A new record. She sat in her car in the driveway, wonder-ing what her move should be. She didn't want to give Luke the idea that she was coming with him, but she wanted to be with him one more time before he left. That was all this was.

Maybe it was stupid. Maybe she should leave well enough alone.

The driver's-side door opened.

"Are you going to sit in there all night or come inside?" Luke looked down at her with the same smile in his eyes, as if nothing had changed. As if he hadn't asked her to give up everything and go with him.

He held out his hand and she took it. He kept her hand as they walked to the house and through the stupid, creaky, bangy screen door. Her heart beat in time with their footsteps as she followed him to his bedroom.

When he closed the door, she turned to face him. "This doesn't mean anything."

"Of course not." Luke sat on the edge of the bed and pulled off his shoes. He wore a pair of flannel pajama pants and no shirt.

Her mouth went dry. "I'm not coming with you to St. Louis."

"That's okay." He stood and moved toward her.

She pressed back into the wall. "I haven't said I love you."

"I know." His tone sounded as if he was trying to calm down a wild animal. He put his hands beside her head on the wall.

"I don't need you. I'm happy with my life the way it is." Her heart pounded harder with every word, knowing that he should be kicking her out.

"And I love you more for it." He leaned in.

She put a hand on his chest to hold him away, knowing he could ignore it if he wanted, but he didn't. "I don't want your love."

"But you have it." He brought his lips to hers and she gave in.

Gave in to the whirlwind of feelings only Luke inspired in her. Gave in to the fact that she wouldn't feel this way with anyone else. Gave in to the press of his lips against hers, his tongue sliding along hers, his heartbeat in time with hers.

She did need him. Her fingers wove in his hair and she pressed her body against his. The warmth of his skin penetrated through her thin layer of clothes. She wanted this night to last forever, but she knew it would end and he'd be gone. Just one last time for closure.

But in truth, she wanted to mark him as hers. Claim him one more time so he'd never forget her. Make him as insane about her as she was about him.

He lifted her shirt, trailing his fingertips across her ribs and along the sides of her breasts. She held her arms up to help him. He pressed his bare chest against hers as her shirt came off. Heat flooded her system and pooled at her core.

His hands rested on her hips as he drew her to him for another kiss. The friction of his skin against hers was setting her system on fire. His fingers stroked along the waistband of her cutoffs until he found the button.

When he rested his forehead against hers, she opened her eyes and met his blue gaze.

"I want you, Luke." *For today, for a month from now, for the rest of my life.* The love she felt for him wouldn't die when he left. She'd probably end up a bitter old woman with just her dog for company.

"There's no one I want more than you." His lips closed over hers. She let his words flow through her. It should be enough that he loved her and wanted her. But something held her back. Even as she gave her body to him fully, she still couldn't give him what he wanted. Trust. Her trust that he wouldn't leave when things got bad. His trust that she wouldn't sleep around.

She shoved the thoughts from her head. Tonight was about saying goodbye. Tomorrow would be soon enough for regrets. He pushed down her cutoffs and slid off his pajama bottoms. With their clothes in a puddle on the floor, he carried her to the bed.

It didn't matter that they'd been together so many times recently. It felt like the first time and the last combined. A hint of discovery as she found a new spot that made him moan and he found a spot that made her hold her breath. And a hint of finality when he entered her. She focused on his eyes, wanting to remember every ounce of pleasure they could wring from each other. And when she came, she cried out his name. Always his and only his. His arms wrapped around her, holding her close to his heart afterward.

Her skin still tingled and her breathing was erratic. She'd never felt more relaxed and at peace than she did in his arms. Her hand rested over his heart. The beating of his corresponded with her own. He pulled her tightly against him and tugged the covers over them.

She shouldn't sleep with him. It was another rule she'd broken for him. She loved to feel him next to her in bed, but she had to give him up in the morning. He'd become a habit that made sleeping without him impossible. She shouldn't let him have that control over her. Wouldn't it be easier to slip out now and avoid the whole scene in the morning anyway?

When she started to rise, his arms pulled her back to him. "Not yet, Penny. I just want to hold you for a little while longer."

Tears gathered in her eyes. She blinked them back. She wanted that, too. "Okay."

"Tell me you won't forget me." Luke's voice was on the edge of sleep.

"Never." Penny could feel the energy draining from her. She just needed a little sleep and then she'd drive back to her place and climb into her cold bed....

"Promise me something." He kissed the top of her head.

"Hmm?" She was so close to sleep. There was nowhere she slept better than in his arms.

"Don't shut me out."

"You're going to be gone," she murmured.

"Not forever. I'll be back." He pulled her against his body until she forgot where she ended and he began. "Promise?"

"Promise."

Luke woke with Penny still in his arms. He smiled at the ceiling. Someday this would be his every day. Penny could take only so much pushing before she closed up entirely. She needed time. He was willing to let her go for now. He could wait for as long as she needed.

She pressed on his chest and propped her head on her hand. "Morning?"

"Yeah." He brushed his knuckles across her cheek.

"I didn't mean to sleep all night." Her smile filled him with relief. Her brown eyes blinked at him, but she wasn't stumbling to get out of bed and away from him.

"I'm glad you did." He scrubbed a hand over his face. "I'd have hated not being able to say goodbye today."

Her brow wrinkled and her fingers curled into him. "I don't like goodbyes."

"How about see-you-soons?"

She pushed up to sitting and brushed her hair from her face. "It'd be better if it weren't a lie."

"It doesn't have to be a lie." He couldn't help the little push; after all, he'd already told her he wanted her to come with him.

"I can't leave here." Penny looked over her shoulder at him. "That's not why I came to see you last night."

He put his hands behind his head. "I know."

If she'd been gearing up for a fight, he didn't have one ready for her. She turned her head away from him. Her slender back was pale with a few freckles. He reached out and followed the trail of freckles with his fingertip.

"If I didn't have to get packed and do chores, I'd spend my last few hours here making love with you."

Her body shuddered beneath his fingers. He breathed in deeply of that scent that was uniquely Penny and smiled. This wasn't goodbye. Things that felt this good didn't end. He would make sure it didn't.

"Do you want me to make breakfast while you do chores?" Penny looked back at him.

In that moment she seemed so vulnerable. He wanted to reassure her that nothing had to change, but she would close up if he did.

"Breakfast would be great." He opened his arms and she snuggled into them. He hugged her to him and kissed her forehead. "Time to start the day."

She nodded against his chest and he could feel the wetness of her tears.

"I love you," he said. "I'm never giving up on you."

She pulled away and searched his eyes. When she opened her mouth—most likely to tell him to stop talking that way—he shoved off the bed and grabbed a pair of underwear.

"Breakfast in twenty?" He pulled on his jeans and a T-shirt.

"Yeah." She still sat on his bed, completely naked except for the sheet she held up.

He brushed her lips with his and left the room. As soon as he reached the kitchen, he took a deep breath in and pushed it out. As much as he wanted to keep her with him, she needed to come to terms with them as a couple first. He might be able to bully her into it with sweet kisses and long nights in his bed, but that wouldn't last.

Something was holding her back. Whether it was because he hadn't trusted her when she tried to manipulate him or whether it went much deeper, she needed to face her fears. He could only let her know that he'd be there when the dust settled.

By the time Luke finished with chores, Brady had arrived. They walked around the farmyard where they'd grown up and talked about what had been taken care of and what still needed to be done.

"So…you and Penny?" Brady pulled a weed from the field and tossed it to the side.

"Hopefully." Luke wasn't used to having his brothers around for advice. Although Brady had been the one to set him straight the summer before senior year.

"Penny's not the same girl she was in high school," Brady said.

Luke couldn't help but smile. "Nope, she's even more magnificent."

"Do you love her?"

Luke stopped and stared at the farmhouse in the distance. Inside, Penny was probably making him breakfast and trying to figure out how to leave without saying goodbye. "Yeah, I love her."

"Maggie said her mother just came back."

"It has messed with her head pretty badly. But she's been dealing with it."

"And you offered to have her come with you?"

Luke started walking toward the farmhouse. "Of course. I love her."

"And what are you giving up for her?"

He stopped dead in his tracks and turned to face Brady. "What do you mean?"

"Love isn't about follow me or don't. It's about finding a happy medium ground. It's about talking through what is best for both your futures. Because it's not just your dreams anymore. It's what you can achieve together."

"I have to finish my rotation—"

"But what about after that? You can't expect her to blindly follow you. I almost lost Maggie by doing that. I thought the only way things would work out was if she and Amber came to New York with me. But the worst thing was going back alone and knowing I'd only get to see them some of the time."

Brady clapped him on the shoulder. "She's got her shop, her best friend and her mother in this town. What are you offering her?"

Brady strode toward the farmhouse, but Luke couldn't move yet. He had done the same thing he did back in high school—made plans for them without realizing that maybe she had plans, too. How stupid could he get? He might as well have drawn a line in the sand and said either come over here with me or stay over there.

Dammit. He needed to fix this now before he lost Penny.

Chapter Twenty-Two

Bacon and eggs and toast. The day was just starting to warm up as Penny stood over the stove. She'd pulled her hair back with a rubber band and used the toothbrush she kept in her purse. She tried her best to cover up the redness around her eyes but kept the rest of her makeup to a minimum.

Luke was leaving again. This time she'd get to say goodbye and good luck. She hoped whoever he ended up with would make him happy. She felt hollow on the inside, but maybe that was for the best. No emotions meant no one could hurt her.

"Morning." Sam came into the kitchen and sat in his chair as if they did this every day.

She plated the over-easy eggs, a couple strips of turkey bacon and two slices of toast. She put it in front of him with a cup of coffee. He grunted.

She was tempted to watch his face when he bit into

the turkey bacon to see if he'd notice the difference, but Brady walked in.

"Hi, Penny." He came over and gave her a one-armed hug, which she shrugged off. "How are things?"

Brady wasn't normally the cuddly type. Because the only thing happening today was Luke leaving, he must be trying to comfort her. Which she didn't need or want.

"Fine." She grabbed a plate and loaded it up for him and shoved it at his chest. "Go eat."

He chuckled and sat at the table.

She finished making two more plates and was about to set them on the table when the door opened. Luke looked out of sorts as he headed for her. She put the plates down and opened her mouth. He grabbed her hand and tugged her after him.

"Breakfast will get cold." She followed after him as he pulled her into his room and shut the door.

"Let it."

"Cold eggs? Not the breakfast of champions." Penny wrinkled her nose.

"Please sit down. I'll make you more eggs." He raked his hand through his hair and paced the room.

She sat on the edge of the bed and waited for whatever he needed to say. What if he was going to try to convince her to go with him? "If you are going to try to convince me to go with you—"

"I'm stupid." He sat next to her.

"Okay. Is that it? We can still make those eggs work…."

"Why do we do this? Every time?" He put his head in his hands.

She rubbed his back. "Whatever is eating you, let it out. I can take it."

He met her eyes. "You can, can't you? Here I was

thinking you needed time to change your mind, but you are the strong one. I get so one-track that I can't see all the other options."

"What are you talking about, Luke?" Her hands trembled as she clasped them in front of her.

"We need to work this out together if it's ever going to work. I can't demand you come to St. Louis with me. We need to make that decision together." He put a hand over hers.

She stood and walked across the room, holding herself tight. "What are you saying?"

"I want us to be together. We can figure out a way to make this work if we really want it."

"Is that what you want?" she said, nervous of what his answer would be and what that would mean to her.

"More than anything."

When she looked into his eyes, she could tell he was being honest, but was it enough?

"I kissed your brother because I knew you'd leave without me." The truth burst out of her before she could stop it. "I knew the rumors of me with other guys bothered you and I hoped you'd believe them if I kissed him. I tore us apart because you will leave me. Everyone I love leaves me."

"I'm not going any—"

"For how long?" She couldn't stop the tears flowing down her cheeks. "A month? A year? Until one of your colleagues gets handsy at the Christmas party? Would you believe me if I said it wasn't my fault? Or would you blame me because I flirt too much?"

"I love—"

"Love isn't enough. You need to trust me."

He grabbed her shoulders and forced her to look up at him. "I trust you. I will believe you always."

"How can I know that?" she whispered.

"I'll spend the rest of my life proving that I trust you, if you'll let me."

She searched those blue eyes she'd always loved. She wanted to believe him. To forget her fears. To not end up alone.

She shook her head. "I can't."

She turned and walked out of his room. She grabbed her purse and said goodbye to Sam and Brady before heading out the door. It closed with a final bang.

Maggie had tried to talk to her about Luke for the past few days, but Penny walked away every time. She just needed to get over him. A few months and she'd be back to her old self and out at the bars, dancing and flirting. Maybe not picking up men....

As she stared out the door of her antiques shop, she rubbed the ache in her chest that had been her constant companion since Luke had left. He'd left himself everywhere she looked. Leaning against the counter while she worked. Teasing her down the aisle while she dusted. Asking her for the story of an old glass bottle.

It wasn't any better at home. Her couch, her kitchen, her dining room, her bedroom. He was everywhere she turned. Every night she'd wait for the doorbell to ring to let her know he was there. But it never did. She lay awake in her bed for hours, trying to ignore the cold spot beside her that still smelled like him.

Penny sighed. It wouldn't be so bad if business weren't so slow. All she had were her thoughts to spin constantly back to Luke.

When the bell over the door rang, she stood and walked around the counter, ready for any distraction.

"I hadn't heard from you in a while." Cheryl walked

over to the counter, all smiles. "I thought I'd pop in and check up on you."

"I'm here." Which was part of the problem. She sank down into a chair.

"What's going on?" Cheryl sat in the chair next to her. "I know I'm not your most favorite person, but I've got a world of experience to share. You can talk to me."

"I don't know what I'm doing." Penny stared out the door at the cars going down Main Street. "I don't know why I can't get over him."

"Man troubles. Was this that handsome man from the other night?" Cheryl leaned back in the chair and crossed her legs.

"Yes." Penny was not at all certain she wanted to talk to Cheryl about this, but maybe she was the best to understand. "I made him leave."

"Why?"

"I hate to blame my messed-up childhood but…" She waved her hand as if she had presented something to her audience.

"It has to be more than that." Cheryl sat quietly for a moment.

Penny wasn't ready to fill in all the blanks.

"Do you love him?"

"Yes." With every fiber of her being.

"Then what's the problem? Doesn't he love you?"

"Yes." Penny stood. "Don't you get it? He loves me and I love him. When he leaves me, I'll be crushed. Alone."

"How is that different than now?" Cheryl said softly.

"I left him! So he couldn't leave me. The first time I made him leave, and this time I left him." She buried her face in her hands.

"If you love him, why did you leave? Was he bad for you? Into drugs? Gambling? Alcohol?"

Penny shook her head. "He would leave me."

"Why, Penny?" her mother pressed.

Penny spun around. "Because you did. Because everyone I ever loved and who claimed to love me leaves and they don't come back."

Cheryl looked down at her hands and took a deep breath. "I'm back now."

"But how can I trust that you won't leave me again? He left me before, so how can I trust he won't do it again?"

"Oh, baby." Tears welled in Cheryl's eyes and trailed down her face. "You have to have faith and let go of your fear. If you don't, you'll just shut everyone out. Wouldn't you rather have a year more with him if it meant you were happy for that year?"

Fear? Faith? "What if he doesn't want me?"

"That's just fear talking." Cheryl stood and put her arm around Penny. "You can't let fear speak for you. Wouldn't it be worse to never see him again? I know I hurt you, Penny. I can't make up for the past, but don't let my problems and my regrets make you not live your life."

"But how do I know?"

Cheryl smiled at her. "You already know. You wouldn't be miserable if you thought you'd done the right thing."

Her mother was making sense. Luke had been pressing her to reveal more of herself, and every fear she'd shown him, he'd held her through. "What do I do?"

"Call him, go to him, get him to come back here or go be with him." Her mother smiled. "I'll be here when you come around."

"But my shop—"

"Won't die without you."

"You won't leave?" The ten-year-old girl inside her needed to hear the words.

"I'm never leaving your life again. No matter what you throw at me. I'm here to support you and need to be part of your life. Even if we aren't in the same town." Cheryl hugged her again, and this time Penny opened her arms and returned the hug.

"Well, then," Penny said, wiping the tears from her eyes, "I need to call Maggie."

Chapter Twenty-Three

Luke finished up his notes in his patient's file. It was quarter past one in the morning, but he knew sleep wouldn't come easily. He'd been back at the hospital for a week, and in that time he'd worked more fiercely than ever to keep his mind from dwelling on Penny.

His first days off weren't for another week, so he couldn't do anything until then. He'd already made plans to go back to Tawnee Valley for that weekend. He wanted to check up on Sam, but mostly he wanted to convince Penny that they belonged together whether it was here or there or anywhere in between.

He scrubbed his hand down his face and stared at the hospital-green walls. He should go home and try to sleep. He was supposed to scrub in on a surgery in the morning.

Stacking his paperwork, he scooted back in his chair,

then grabbed his keys. As he headed to the elevator, a nurse called out to him.

"Doctor Ward?"

Luke walked toward the nurse. "What is it?"

"Someone's here to see you." The nurse glanced down the hallway.

"At this hour?"

She nodded. "I put her in room twenty."

"Thanks." Luke grabbed a cup of coffee from the nurse's station and went to the room she'd indicated. "How can I hel—"

Sitting on the bed was Penny. "Hi."

Luke closed the door and crossed the room to stand before her, but he didn't touch her, afraid she wouldn't be real. "What are you— When did you—"

"Cat got your tongue?" Penny swung her crossed leg. "Never thought I'd make Luke Ward speechless. Where are your color-coded index cards when you need them?"

"I missed you." Luke's pulse raced. She'd come to him.

"I missed you, too." She pushed her hair behind her ear. "So, *Doctor,* I've been having these pains right here." She pressed her hand to her chest.

"Is that so?" He wanted to reach out and touch her so badly, but he held himself back. If he touched her, he wouldn't stop until they were both naked.

"It started before you left." Her brown eyes held his gaze. "I don't think I ever stopped loving you. I was so scared that you would leave me that I didn't want to give you that power over my heart. You left so easily the last time—"

"Because I was scared, too. I loved you so much it hurt and seeing you with Sam did a number on me.

But I think you knew that. Otherwise you would have picked any other guy to kiss."

"I'm sorry."

"I don't need you to be sorry. I need you to have a little faith in me and trust that I won't ever intentionally try to hurt you."

"I couldn't help trying to drive you away this time, too...."

"It didn't work. I was planning on coming back to you every chance I got. Even if it was just to get inside your bedroom for a day or two, I knew eventually I'd win you over. You make my life fun and sexy. You remind me of the man I am when my logical side wants to take over. I want you with me for as long as you'll have me. If I thought you'd say yes to marrying me, I'd fly us to Vegas on the next flight out."

She smiled and reached out to hold his face. "Someday on the marriage thing. First, let's try to make this work. You make the fear worthwhile. You make it easy to forget to be afraid. Are you ready to trust me?"

He lowered his mouth until just a hair's breadth was between them. "With my life and with my heart. I love you, Penny."

"I love you, Luke." She pressed her lips to his, sealing their love with perfection.

* * * * *

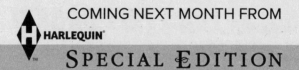

REQUEST YOUR FREE BOOKS!

2 FREE NOVELS PLUS 2 FREE GIFTS!

❤ HARLEQUIN®

SPECIAL EDITION

Life, Love & Family

YES! Please send me 2 FREE Harlequin® Special Edition novels and my 2 FREE gifts (gifts are worth about $10). After receiving them, if I don't wish to receive any more books, I can return the shipping statement marked "cancel." If I don't cancel, I will receive 6 brand-new novels every month and be billed just $4.74 per book in the U.S. or $5.24 per book in Canada. That's a savings of at least 14% off the cover price! It's quite a bargain! Shipping and handling is just 50¢ per book in the U.S. and 75¢ per book in Canada.* I understand that accepting the 2 free books and gifts places me under no obligation to buy anything. I can always return a shipment and cancel at any time. Even if I never buy another book, the two free books and gifts are mine to keep forever.

235/335 HDN F45Y

Name	(PLEASE PRINT)

Address	Apt. #

City	State/Prov.	Zip/Postal Code

Signature (if under 18, a parent or guardian must sign)

Mail to the Harlequin® Reader Service:
IN U.S.A.: P.O. Box 1867, Buffalo, NY 14240-1867
IN CANADA: P.O. Box 609, Fort Erie, Ontario L2A 5X3

Want to try two free books from another line?
Call 1-800-873-8635 or visit www.ReaderService.com.

* Terms and prices subject to change without notice. Prices do not include applicable taxes. Sales tax applicable in N.Y. Canadian residents will be charged applicable taxes. Offer not valid in Quebec. This offer is limited to one order per household. Not valid for current subscribers to Harlequin Special Edition books. All orders subject to credit approval. Credit or debit balances in a customer's account(s) may be offset by any other outstanding balance owed by or to the customer. Please allow 4 to 6 weeks for delivery. Offer available while quantities last.

Your Privacy—The Harlequin® Reader Service is committed to protecting your privacy. Our Privacy Policy is available online at www.ReaderService.com or upon request from the Harlequin Reader Service.

We make a portion of our mailing list available to reputable third parties that offer products we believe may interest you. If you prefer that we not exchange your name with third parties, or if you wish to clarify or modify your communication preferences, please visit us at www.ReaderService.com/consumerchoice or write to us at Harlequin Reader Service Preference Service, P.O. Box 9062, Buffalo, NY 14269. Include your complete name and address.

HSE13R

Read on for a sneak peek at
New York Times *bestselling author Allison Leigh's*
A WEAVER CHRISTMAS GIFT, the latest in
THE RETURN TO THE DOUBLE C *miniseries.*

*Jane Cohen's ready for a baby. There's just one thing
missing—the perfect guy. Unfortunately, the only one
she wants is tech wiz Casey Clay, but kids definitely
aren't on his radar. Can Jane create the family she's
always dreamed of with the secretive, yet sexy, Casey?*

***

She exhaled noisily and collapsed on the other end of the
couch. "Casey—"

"I just wanted to see you."

She slowly closed her mouth, absorbing that. Her fingers
tightened around the glass. She could have offered him one.
He'd been the one to introduce her to that particular winery
in the first place. The first time she'd invited him to her place
after they'd moved their relationship into the "benefits"
category, he'd brought a bottle of wine.

She'd been wholly unnerved by it and told him they
weren't dating—just mutually filling a need—and to save
the empty romantic gestures.

He hadn't brought a bottle of wine ever again.

She shook off the memory.

He was here now, in her home, uninvited, and she'd be
smart to remember that. "Why?"

He pushed off the couch and prowled around her living room. He'd always been intense. But she'd never really seen him *tense*. And she realized she was seeing it now.

She slowly sat forward and set her glass on the coffee table, watching him. "Casey, what's wrong?"

He shoved his fingers through his hair, not answering. Instead, he stopped in front of a photo collage on the wall above her narrow bookcase that Julia had given her last Christmas. "You going to go out with him again?"

Something ached inside her. "Probably," she admitted after a moment.

"He's a good guy," he muttered. "A little straightlaced, but otherwise okay."

She didn't know what was going on with him. But she suddenly felt like crying, and Jane wasn't a person who cried. "Casey."

"You could do worse." Then he gave her a tight smile and walked out of the living room into the kitchen. A second later, she heard the sound of her back door opening and closing.

He couldn't have left her more bewildered if he'd tried.

***

Find out what happens next in
New York Times *bestselling author Allison Leigh's*
A WEAVER CHRISTMAS GIFT, the latest in
THE RETURN TO THE DOUBLE C *miniseries.*

Available November 2014 from
Harlequin® Special Edition.

H HARLEQUIN®

SPECIAL EDITION

Life, Love and Family

Coming in November 2014

THE SOLDIER'S HOLIDAY HOMECOMING

by *USA TODAY* bestselling author

Judy Duarte

Sergeant Joe Wilcox is back where he never
expected to be—Brighton Valley, which he left
long ago. He's in town because he promised
to deliver a letter for a fellow marine to
Chloe Dawson, who broke his late pal's heart.
But before he can do so, Joe is struck by a car and
gets temporary amnesia. Joe can't remember who
he is, but he's intrigued by the lovely Chloe.
Can the soldier and his sweetheart find
happily-ever-after just in time for Christmas?

Don't miss the latest edition of the
***Return to Brighton Valley* miniseries!**

Available wherever books and ebooks are sold.

www.Harlequin.com

HSE65849